THE SPARE ROOM

Of Elves and Men

THE SPARE ROOM

Of Elves and Men

P R BROWN

By the same author:

Non-fiction

The Gods of Our Time

Dreams and Illusions Revisited

The Mountain Dwellers

Fiction

The Mirror Men

The Treadmillers

The Shadow People

Circle Walker

Diary of the Last Man

First published 2023 by DB Publishing, an imprint of JMD Media Ltd, Nottingham, United Kingdom.

ISBN 9781780916347

Printed in the UK

Elves and men, it might be said,
Abide in worlds apart.
But time and tide may yet dictate
A common bond, a brand new start ...

... Until then, the Elves, painfully aware of man's fateful limitations, await a shared enlightenment – they await with an infinity of patience that only they possess, knowing that time and tide can never be coerced. The contemptuous, violent, even murderous, antagonism between religions, for example, is grounded in this, that benevolent gods make the best of men in their image, while the worst of men make malevolent gods in theirs. Enlightenment, though hanging by a single thread, comes when all men know which gods are which, which to praise, which to abjure, which to love, which to revile ...

... When all is rightly said and done,
Egregious gods will fade away,
As, in early morning's warming sun,
The frost is loathe to stay.

CONTENTS

Chapter One

ABOUT ELVES

Why I walked into our spare room, I can't for the life of me say. I suppose I must have gone there for some reason. But it often happens with humans, of which I am apologetically one, that they do things and then can't say for the life of them why they did them, except to say that something seemed like a good idea at the time. In any case, this fault is not one shared by the Wood Elves, for they always have a reason, the very best of reasons, for everything they do, and they always know why they do what they do.

(By the way, Wood Elves are so called, not because they are made of wood, which would be silly and disrespectful, and also bad grammar, because then it would have been better to say that they are 'wooden Elves' , but because they live in and amongst trees in woods and forests, and quite often even in woods which happen to border houses. You may well ask why they are not called Tree Elves. For the life of me I have no satisfactory answer, except to say that even Mr Potts (now sadly deceased) of whom you will hear a great deal later and who was, in a very odd way, in communication with them, could furnish no explanation above and beyond the acute observation that the existence of a wood implies the existence of trees but not the other way round. In other words, a few trees do not make a wood, but a wood is made up of many. I don't find this entirely satisfactory and neither did my friend Mr Potts, but it will really have to do, at least until the Elves themselves deign to explain otherwise. Well, I suppose the logic of the explanation is sound enough. After all, a bachelor is a man, but a man is not necessarily a bachelor – which, of course, has nothing to do with Elves! Well, anyway, *you* may call them Tree Elves, let your conscience dictate what it might, but Mr Potts would have had none of it, and I have come to respect his position on most things, so that's that. As far as I know and care, they are Wood Elves.)

Well, when I walked into our spare room, not knowing why I had done so, I noticed that the bed was lumpy. Most spare rooms have beds. A bed may be lumpy some of the time, but not all of the time, and I think we can safely say that not all beds are lumpy all of the time and that some beds are never lumpy. A bed is not lumpy when it isn't used. And that's why I was surprised to find that the bed in the spare room was lumpy, because we had no guests staying with us. The bed in the spare room should have been quite flat, because no one was expected to be sleeping in it. And no head was visible on or anywhere near the pillow.

When I bent over the bed to check, I found that no one *was* sleeping in it, that it was perfectly empty, as it should have been. Yes – but the fact that the bed was mysteriously lumpy set me thinking about Wood Elves.

I must explain.

Wood Elves sleep in trees or on the ground under blankets of leaves. Sometimes, though, they have been known to snatch bed sheets from washing lines when no one is looking. This is not exactly stealing, for in Elvish there is no word for it. Instead, it's called 'fletching', which, loosely translated, means 'borrowing without permission'. After all, Elves, being Elves, can't be seen by humans without the risk of being mistaken for other humans, which would never do! They naturally keep a very low profile. But the bed sheets are always returned to the washing lines, not only spick and span but even cleaner than they were before, which is why humans are so often pleased with the aroma of their washing when it seems much sweeter than it does in the usual wash.

But why, you ask, do Elves want to 'borrow' the sheets in the first place? A good question. The answer is partly because Elves, being Elves, are often up to mischief, just for the sake of it, you understand. For them, it's just a bit of fun. But also, there is an old Elvish saying: 'A new sheet is as good as a change, and a change is as good as a new leaf'. I must confess, I have never been able to make sense of this old saying, but it clearly makes sense to them. Anyway, after taking a sheet, an Elf will normally lie under it for a night, after covering it with leaves. If he didn't cover it with leaves, it would stand out in the moonlight and attract the wrong kind of attention. During the night, he would, like humans, move in his sleep, and if you happened to be in the vicinity, which is most unlikely, you would put down his movements to the wind rustling the leaves, except when there is no wind, in which case you might think it's some kind of magic and be alarmed, and, if there were an owl about and owls could speak, it would tell you that there's no cause for alarm at all because it's just an Elf turning over in bed.

Building houses very close to big trees, especially woods and forests, may on occasion inspire Elves not only to snatch bed sheets from washing lines but to actually enter a house in the middle of the night and sleep in a spare room – a very risky undertaking for the chances of being found out there and then are very great. That is why I was especially interested in the lumpy bed, though heaven knows what I would have done had I found an Elf lying there, or what he would have done. He would probably have uttered something in Elvish which I had no chance of understanding, and then leapt out of the window towards the woods beyond with a skip, a hop and a jump.

Now it's perfectly true that no one can actually look at an Elf, if only because Elves are too quick to move out of sight and don't want to be seen however much humans want to see them.

But there really was a time when, on the later and unimpeachable authority of Mr Potts himself, I actually caught a glimpse of an Elf – well, actually, it was quite a long glimpse, if there is ever such a thing as a long glimpse. It was a She-Elf, dressed in the usual mossy green clothes; her eyes were summer-sky blue, and her hair was a golden as the sun, and on her head she wore a green hat like the upside down cap of an acorn, and she was as slim and lithe as a branch of a tender tree. Her skin was clear and radiant. I must confess, I thought her a most beautiful creature. But I dared not approach her or in any way make known that she was seen. In another instant she was gone, gone forever, like someone you meet in a dream and never see or dream of again. But, as you see, she has stayed with me all this time, in the shape of a memory, half but not completely forgotten, and her beauty has saved me from the worst that I might have become. It's as though I have always hoped I'd see her again, and then maybe of approaching her and talking to her and ... Ah! But all this is quite hopeless, because, as you must appreciate, the world of Elves is quite different from that of humans. Elves would never willingly communicate with humans, because they know that to do so is quite fruitless, since they are quite incapable of lasting peace and are forever quarrelling about this or that. More than this, humans do not live forever while Elves are eternal beings, which means that they understand worlds past and, because they understands worlds past, they also understand the present and even worlds to come – worlds to come, because the worlds to come are not so different from the worlds that have been, for humans learn so slowly or even not at all. Elves have a saying about humans: look to the past and you will see the future – and I suppose this is because humans never change, at least not very much and hardly ever for the better. It pains Elves to see how humans treat trees, which are especially beloved, cutting them down and rarely replacing them. If humans go on like this, the time will surely come when Elves will have no forests to live in. So, you can't really expect them to show much respect for humans and their horrid ways.

Well, anyway, I never saw that She-Elf again, except in dreams from time to time – strangely, now I come to think of it, at times when I *needed* to dream of her. Of course, Elves would never have anything to do with humans on a personal level. An Elf could never ever marry a human, for example. It would be most odd to see an Elf sitting at a table in a fast food restaurant or standing in a queue waiting for a bus, or cheering in a football crowd. So I never thought for one moment that I could actually do with that She-Elf the things that people normally do when they are together, and I never expected by some chance to see her on the top of a double-decker bus or strolling through a shopping centre. There could be no 'normal' sighting of her, and no communication of the kind that most people would call 'normal'. Perhaps she was a kind of guardian angel, since she could be nothing else. And although she looked very young and sprite, she might well have been as old as the hills, because Elves age very slowly, not like humans, who feel bitter about the passing of the years and the appearance of wrinkles – if humans spot a new wrinkle in the mirror, it can spoil their whole day and make them angry with the whole world and each other. Elves are not like that; in any case, they never look into mirrors, because they haven't any, and no self-respecting Elf would want one either. Yes, they are very different from humans! And yet, not *totally* different either.

Chapter Two

ABOUT MR POTTS

Being a very astute reader, as you most certainly are, you are bound to ask how it is that I should know anything at all about Elves – if Elves are never seen or heard, and if the world of Elves is quite different from that of humans. How on earth could I set myself up as an authority on Elves? Well, of course, I am not an authority on Elves, but the little I know about them comes from dreams, though, alas alack, not my *own* dreams, yes *dreams*! – you know, those little experiences we have while asleep. For this is the only way the Elves dare to make themselves known to the world of humans. And even then they are quite selective. They won't appear to anyone who refuses to believe that they exist. Nor will they appear to those who take axes to trees without even a second thought. Unlike humans, they will not try to influence someone they believe to be beyond a change of heart. Your mind needs to be open to them, for only then will it be possible to dream the kind of dream that is a door to them. A dream is a door an Elf walks through to make themselves known. If someone is apt to dream dreams of dark and nasty places full or horror and monsters, dreams so full of fear that there's no room left for anything else – well, an Elf will not appear in such dreams. Such horrible dreams are like locked doors, doors that will not open even though there are no bolts and no locks to pick. Elves will only enter through doors that open easily with the slightest push of their very slender fingers.

And so, not everyone will know Elves in dreams – and if they can't know them in dreams, it follows from what I have said that they will never know them at all.

It also follows that I can't have met Elves in dreams – I mean, not me personally. For my dreams tend to be horrid, dark and dreary – that is, when I dream at all, which is not all that often. My library of dreams is full of heavy, musty tomes that no one would ever wish to read. No, I must be very honest and say that I have never met Elves in any of my dreams, not even a solitary Elf. Of course, I wish I had the kind of dreams that would make it possible. No matter, for what I know of Elves comes directly from Mr Potts and *his* dreams.

Mr Potts was just the sort of person able to dream of Elves. I must tell you about him, if only to dispel some nasty, hurtful rumours circulating about the poor fellow. Well, it's perfectly true that old Mr Potts had become a bit odd, but I put that down to his age and because he lived quite alone. His wife had died many years ago, and his two children, both grown up and living in other countries, seldom wrote to him and never visited. They'd promised to visit him at Christmas time, but they'd been making the same promise for years, although he still told everyone, when every Christmas approached, that they'd be coming and that he'd be very busy making all the preparations for their visit. He had said this so many times that he actually believed it. But, thankfully, between Christmases he managed to forget all about it and got on with his simple life of eating and sleeping and tending his flowers in his small garden.

Yes, he did have his odd ways. His little house still stands alone in a leafy lane, and, when leaving it to go shopping, he returns to the front door several times to make sure that he had locked it behind him. He would press the door with the palm of his hand to make sure of it. He had even been known to unlock the door again to assure himself that it was locked in the first place. One of his neighbours, not a very nice lady, had watched him doing this and gossiped and joked about it. On one occasion she laughed so much she almost choked on the plum she was scoffing, which would have been good riddance – to her, not the plum. But she didn't choke and never learned a lesson from it, and so she goes on gossiping about Mr Potts's odd behaviour even now. Trouble is, Mr Potts's behaviour did encourage that kind of gossip. His doubts about the front door were not the only problem. He had been seen treating the garden gate in the same way. Having begun to walk down the lane, he would be seen to return several times to check that the gate had been properly closed. He would actually open the gate and then walk up the path to the front door, unlock it, lock it again, walk through the gate, close it and make his way down the lane again only to return and repeat the whole thing over, which gave rise to remarks like, 'It's a wonder he manages to do any shopping at all!' which were never meant kindly.

And when he did manage to get to the shops he was known to dither for ages over what sort of cheese he should buy or whether he should buy white bread or brown bread or go for something, to use his own phrase, 'foreign-looking'. The local shopkeepers tried their best not to show their irritation, but at times it was very hard to conceal. Strangely though, he had no such problem about clothes – clothes didn't seem to matter to him, which of course means that his appearance was often thought to be as dotty as he was. He just threw something on to cover his skin. If it was cold he wore a thick coat. If it was warm, a thin coat. The only item of clothing he cared much about was his hat. He had just one hat, a battered and moth-eaten fedora, and just wouldn't leave the house without it whatever the state of the weather. In very cold weather he would wear it indoors. 'I wouldn't be at all surprised if you wore it in bed as well!' I once joked in the early days of our friendship. He just turned away without so much as a smile, from which I felt inclined to deduce that he did, in fact, wear it in bed – I was also determined to be extremely careful in future about the jokes I was tempted to make!

The result of all this is that he had acquired, thankfully unknown to himself, the title 'Potty Potts'. I say 'thankfully' because it might have hurt his feelings, and of course I myself said nothing at all to him about such stuff. I regarded him as a friend and as a very decent sort. Besides, he was my only source of information about Elves, and I had no wish to threaten that source by offending him unnecessarily.

The thing about Mr Potts is that there was none of this dithering nonsense about sleeping. In short, he slept like a baby. And as for bad dreams, he was entirely free of them. 'I put my head on the pillow,' he once told me, 'and I'm away!' He meant, of course, that he had no trouble at all getting to sleep and staying asleep until the birds sang in the early morning, though sometimes he woke so early that the birds were still asleep and in danger of falling headlong in a sleepy stupor from the branches of the big tree outside Mr Potts's bedroom window. His ability to fall asleep so quickly and sleep so soundly was of course a great gift. He didn't need to count sheep and get confused in the process. He didn't need to read and read until the book crashed like a spare cannon ball onto his bedroom floor and wake him up again. No, he needed none of these well-known aids to get to sleep.

(It's just as well to note here that when I say Mr Potts didn't need to 'count sheep', I am not talking about *real* sheep and counting them as a farmer might count them to see that they're all there. The expression 'to count sheep' means only to count *imaginary* sheep in an attempt to make yourself feel sleepy.

I shall make notes of this kind from time to time, because, following Mr Potts's example, it's most important to ensure that people understand what you mean and that they don't imagine that you mean something entirely different – not only entirely different, but often quite ridiculous!)

But more important than Mr Potts's getting to sleep instantly and his staying asleep was his remarkable ability to dream of Elves.

Chapter Three

ABOUT DREAMS

Mr Potts dreamed of Elves. I suppose they must have spoken to him in his dreams, after deciding to speak to him in a language he could understand, because they told him they were watching and waiting in the trees and were often mistaken for large birds like crows and such like, and, because humans found it hard to believe in anything other than power, money, fame, ambition and, above all, themselves, they never thought to question whether what they thought were crows rustling their feathers and cawing on the treetops and in the dense branches were anything other than crows, plain and simple.

(I say 'plain and simple', but I'm not at all sure that anything in this whole wide world is plain and simple. And even if it's plain and simple to you, it may not be plain and simple to someone else! The mind boggles, and the vast majority of minds hate boggling – it's most upsetting and is no recipe at all for harmonious living.)

Mr Potts also told me that Elves are very *logical* creatures, because they refuse to hope for anything, let alone *expect* anything, that doesn't make sense. They know, he said, that hope is a great source of strength. But it's no use hoping for something that can't possibly come about, like, for example, a round square. Something may be round, or something may be square, but it can't at the same time be both round and square, or it would be like saying that Mr Potts has locked the front door and that he hasn't, or that an egg is a banana or that a banana is an egg – although of course there are many humans who might *say* things and even *believe* things which are just as silly as that.

So, Elves only hope for things that are possible, which means to say that there should also be a very good reason for hoping. And it would be no use talking to them about having something called Faith, if that meant having it without good reason. Elves are not what humans might call 'religious'. No, not at all.

So they watch and they wait. I asked Mr Potts what they could possibly be waiting for. He explained that they observe good people and they observe bad people, that they see good things and bad things. And although they see bad far more often than they see good, they believe that the good they see is a good enough reason for hoping to see much more good than bad *eventually*, and even, one day, to see no more bad at all. They notice, he said, the little acts of kindness that some people perform for one another and they are very impressed – so much so that they hope for the time when all acts are acts of kindness.

As for Mr Potts himself, he believed the Elves are over-impressed and far too hopeful. He did not share their hopes. And so, although he was very content, he can't be said to have been happy. And they are not at all the same, you know - I mean, being happy and being content. He hoped for nothing and expected nothing. He shocked me once when he said that it took a certain kind of courage to give up your hopes. I'm afraid it really sounded as though poor Mr Potts himself had given up on mankind big-time.

On the other hand, and judging by his ability to fall asleep so easily and to stay asleep until the small birds start tweeting in the mists of early morning, there may after all be something to be said for a life without expectation and without hope. Such a life may not after all be – well, shall we say, *entirely* unhappy? Does this sound contradictory – being happy and at the same time without hope? Yet, Mr Potts taught me that some contradictions are worth their weight in gold and shouldn't, therefore, be rejected without a second thought.

('Worth their weight in gold' only means that some contradictions are very valuable. This expression is figurative and intends no reference to the real precious metal, which I'm sure you know already.)

And the fact that Mr Potts's dreams were without the horrors and pains and sorrows of hopes repeatedly dashed meant that they were open doors for Elves. Elves, you might say, felt a certain affinity with Mr Potts – they were kindred spirits, as it were.

While they watched and waited they had at least found one human with whom they felt they could communicate, though, of course, the communication was only one way and, out of very exceptional consideration for Mr Potts, in a language he could understand. You might say, Elves spoke *to* him, but not *with* him.

It must be emphasised in case I have not already made it quite clear that while Mr Potts could not have been described as a happy man in any regular sense, he was quite content. And it's not that he had any bad thoughts at all about humans, any more than he had good ones. All such thoughts, good or bad, stopped bothering him long ago. He gave them up, or perhaps they gave *him* up. Concerning human affairs he had, you might say, a blank mind, like a book full of empty pages. There had been a time, long ago, when he expected the best in human affairs. When his expectations failed to be met, he resorted instead to hoping for the best. And finally he believed the best course of action is not to think about human affairs at all, which was why he never read newspapers or listened to the news. He listened to music on his antiquated radio, *very* selectively, but he switched off as soon as anything came up concerning political matters, which was, and still is of course, more often than not.

Any outsider would have considered Mr Potts a man of the strictest routine. His daily schedule was nothing but robotic. He was, you might say, a creature of strict habit. This is a subject of fascination for the Elves, for their habits are anything but strict, according to Mr Potts, that is. Perhaps the Elves had talked about it amongst themselves and decided that Mr Potts was a very fit subject for observation. Maybe they talked about it amongst themselves in his dreams, and with such wonder and amusement that they spoke in whispers. He heard them say that more than one Elf had fallen out of their trees with laughter. But some Elves do have a very serious side to them as well, one of the Elves suggesting that perhaps Mr Potts was protecting himself from something by being so strict and unbending about his daily routine. The idea was immediately dropped, because it was met with even more peals of laughter as a few more Elves lost their balance and fell headlong onto the grassy carpet below. Well, it seems you can't be too serious for too long if you're an Elf – you have to work yourself up to it by degrees.

Chapter Four

THE ROMAN SENATE

Whether or not the Elf who had made the suggestion which caused more Elves to fall off their branches with laughter was right about Mr Potts, somehow shielding himself with an unshakeable routine, there is little doubt that an unvaried routine can make you rather foolish. Those who like to impress others with a little knowledge of words have been heard to say that a fixed routine is 'stultifying', a word which comes from the Latin 'stultus', which means 'stupid'. If you do the same thing at the same time often enough, it might happen that you *think* you've done it when you *haven't*. For example, if you take a shower every morning with keen regularity, there just might come a morning when you would swear that you've taken it when in fact you haven't. Or, if you lock your front door every morning before walking away down your garden path, there might come a morning when in fact you've left it *un*locked. Why? Because you mistakenly assume that you locked it, and your assumption is based on what you have, until now, unfailingly done.

If this makes sense to you, and you may be sure that there are many for whom it will make no sense at all, it might help to explain Mr Potts's obsessive behaviour. It's as though he didn't trust his own routine, or didn't trust himself to stick to it, or perhaps it's because he vaguely understood that a routine can be *stultifying*. Anyway, Mr Potts's strict routine did leave something to be desired, because it seemed to confuse him and make him the butt of jokes amongst both Elves and humans. You might even say that his routine turned in on itself – like an in-growing toenail. Speaking of toenails, it was also part of his routine to cut them every Friday evening before toddling off to bed. You will not be surprised to know that he sometimes forgot to do it, thinking that he'd done it already, or that he sometimes did it twice, consequently cutting them down too much and hobbling about for two or three days in pain and speculating about possible causes.

In any event, his routine often got the better of him, and in ways which are beyond doubt very humorous – which might explain why the Elves went out of their way to observe his antics and were frequently in stitches – if only humans had believed in Elves sufficiently to hear them chortling and guffawing away! Some of Mr Potts's antics have already been mentioned. But we may pause to recount one or two more.

It can happen that you not only forget to do what you think you've already done, but that you do again the very thing that you've done already, just like the over-cutting of toenails mentioned. On more than one occasion, Mr Potts had undressed and dipped his toe into his bath only to exclaim, 'Silly me. I've done this already!' He would get out of the bath and dress again, little realising that he hadn't taken a bath at all that morning. Since he always kept the bathroom window open for fresh air, the Elves saw everything from their elevated positions and, of course, laughed their heads off – an event Mr Potts failed to notice, being too busy dressing again and muttering to himself how foolish he was. It must be stressed that Mr Potts, being a firm believer in the existence of Elves, would be capable of hearing them chuckling away if he had managed to get close enough and wasn't too distracted by self-criticism. He *never* got close enough and was *always* distracted by self-criticism.

(When I say the Elves laughed their heads off, I am not to be taken literally. There are few things more disconcerting than the image of headless Elves – almost as unacceptable as headless movie stars. I mean, of course, that they laughed a lot. No more than that, thank goodness.)

I have said that Mr Potts, though not happy, was quite content. True, he seemed to have freed himself from the hopes and expectations that concern human affairs, which explains why he slept so soundly and unworriedly that Elves were able to enter his dreams with ease. Yet, it seems that his routine wasn't really enough to entertain his waking mind. He has adopted another kind of eccentricity to fill the gap – and that was his very deep interest in the past, so deep in fact that if the past was an ocean he would have sunk out of sight! I suppose his interest in the past was perfectly understandable, given his long-standing dissatisfaction with the present. He'd heard the joke that there's no future in the past – but as long as the past didn't contain the present, the past was quite alright with him. Mr Potts had read widely about past events, most of them depressing events, of course. But, the way he saw it, at least they were over and done with. 'The very idea of travelling back in time in a time machine and witnessing again all those terrible things would be a living nightmare without equal. It is quite enough to read about them!', Mr Potts once told me, as we took a turn round his garden. 'If only they could all have been avoided!' he added, with a sigh and gesturing skyward, as though the answer lay somewhere among the clouds.

Feeling entirely unable to do anything about the present, it's as though he imagined he might have had a better chance of changing the past had he been *there* in the past instead of *here* in the present. Now, as absurd as that sounds, and it *sounds* absurd precisely because it *is* absurd, it might nonetheless explain quite nicely the ridiculous event I experienced when I dropped in on Mr Potts – as I did regularly, once or twice a week, depending on the weather.

Ringing the doorbell without a response, I naturally assumed he'd slipped to the shops, and I was about to walk away down the garden path when I heard a voice or voices which seem to come from the rear garden, and so I made my way there, thinking perhaps he was home after all.

I was startled to find Mr Potts standing in the middle of his garden loudly pontificating towards the tall Copper Beech and Sycamore trees which stand like inert sentinels above and in front of the dilapidated wooden garden fence that formed the perimeter of Mr Potts's large lawn and continued along the backs of neighbouring houses. He stood with his back to me, quite unaware that anyone was there. A large curtain was wrapped round him in the manner of a toga, leaving his left arm and shoulder bare, and on his head was a leafy headband, clearly homemade because some of the leaves, a little worse for wear, were drooping despairingly over one eye. He seemed to imagine that the Copper Beeches were senators in the Roman Senate and that it was his turn to speak his mind on the occasion of some momentous or tragic event, exactly *what* I never managed to ascertain, and that to make his mark he would need to hold forth in stentorian tones with no shilly-shallying and firing on all cylinders by borrowing a little from William Shakespeare and throwing a little Bob Dylan into the mix, just for starters:

'*Friends, Romans, Countrymen, lend me your ears! You may well rise from your seats and stand in my presence! For times are changing and we must heed the call, so don't stand round or sit on your haunches but listen to reason and the voice of virtue, not that I count myself the fount of all wisdom, mind you. But so much bad stuff is coming which can be avoided with a little restraint, a little wisdom and kind hearts. My advice to you is to heed the warning of your esteemed Augustus and limit the expansion of the Empire. In other words, stop meddling in other countries – you will not be thanked for it. You will, quite rightly, be met with fierce resistance, scorn, contempt and derision, and, after the defeat of Rome, which will most certainly come about, every Roman colony, province and 'civitas' will revert to its former primitive condition through barbarism and ignorance and neglect, through a level of stupidity so great that even domestic central heating, your wonderful 'hypocaust', will not be re-invented for another 1,500 years after your decline. Only the bad things will be remembered and the good things left to decay, all the good that you do will be left to rack and ruin. You will be said to have done more harm than good. No, no, limit your Empire, curb your expansionism, but increase your legions and protect the borderlands of this great city from the barbaric hoards without. Look inward! Try much harder to remove the poverty from your own streets, for it's not enough to be blessed with Roman citizenship if you still live in abject poverty as so many Romans do. The housing and streets in the poorer quarters are a disgrace and need a great clean-up. In short, mind your own business, strengthen your defences and improve the quality of life of every citizen – and as for slaves, do please give them their freedom, make them all citizens, educate them and give them skills and jobs with a good living wage. I remind you of your own SPQR, which we find everywhere – 'Senatus Populusque Romanus'. The Senate doesn't stand alone but is the representative and guardian of the people – so it's fitting that you should represent and guard them, and you do this by doing right by them.*

For these things you will be remembered far more kindly. And another thing ...'

I didn't stay around to discover what that other thing was. Since he hadn't seen me during all this time, I decided to sneak away and leave him to it. To interrupt him would have been rude, and embarrassing to us both. In any case, I was not a member of that imaginary Senate and was present without invitation. He seemed to be working himself up to a climax. Mr Potts may not have had the eloquence of Cicero, but he felt he had something to say and was determined to say it, although whether what he said made any sense I am quite unable to say. His mention of central heating seemed odd to me – but, there we are, I am no authority and such is the price of ignorance. So, I took a few steps backward gingerly and then walked back down the garden path and away.

I found myself asking repeatedly whether Mr Potts was truly barking mad or just an amusing eccentric, and I can't decide which to this day. Did he really and truly think he was addressing his Elves in the branches of the Copper Beeches and the Sycamores, thinking them to be members of the Senate of ancient Rome? Whether temporarily insane or just eccentric, it was taking things a bit too far. It was just as well that it was me and not the local gossips who had witnessed his address to that august but imaginary assembly.

(Incidentally, and just in case you are wondering, 'august' means 'distinguished' and not the month after July and before September. The month is spelt with a capital 'A' – but of course you know this.)

Mr Potts's fascination with the past, as a soothing, even necessary and inevitable, diversion from the present, had led him to read widely. No-one, I should hazard to say, had made more frequent and fruitful use of the local library than he.

It's curious, though, that he should have imagined addressing the Senate of ancient Rome in an attempt to warn of disasters in the wake of Roman expansionism, while at the same time not seeming to take any interest in the affairs of his own time. This is what some might call a paradox. The word 'paradox' is quite hopeful, because it seems to suggest that there's an explanation if only we have the patience to look for it and the wherewithal to find it. My own explanation is that, for Mr Potts, both the present and the past were and are lost causes, and that by addressing the past he was, somewhere in the deep, dark recesses of his mind, acknowledging that there is as much hope of righting the wrongs of the present as there is of changing the past, and so, he might as well address the past as the present – in either case, hope was useless, as useless as finding a square circle or a circular square.

I never let on to Mr Potts that I had witnessed his speech to the Senate. But I did wonder whether he had made or was planning to make similar speeches in different periods of history. I have imagined him making pointless overtures to dictators like Franco, Mussolini and Hitler under the tall Copper Beeches and the Sycamores. I don't know whether he had extended his historical repertoire in this way, but I remember him telling me that the Elves in his dreams regularly spoke amongst themselves of his crazily useless efforts to right past wrongs when he seemed to care less than nothing about the present state of the world. I confess I had made no sense of this at all – until, that is, I witnessed his speech to the imaginary Senate of ancient Rome. It's odd how one piece of insanity can explain another, how one error can, let's say, be grounded in another – you could even imagine a pyramid of errors, and there are a great many such pyramids about far more imposing and problematic than their Egyptian counterparts. It struck me that the present is made up of the past, that what humans have done in the past lays the groundwork or the template, as it were, for the present, just as what humans do in the present lays the groundwork or the template for the future – which, perhaps, is just another way of saying that what humans do, good or bad, changes little over the centuries. Hmm, but I'm never sure of the authority of my own thoughts, and have preferred to defer to those of Mr Potts instead.

I think I should take this opportunity to clarify what perhaps is already clear enough but which even so needs to be emphasised. To use rather large words, because it's not easy to use short ones, we must say that *acceptance* is not at all the same as *agreement*, or we might say that *resignation* is not at all the same as *approval*. Now, what I mean is, Mr Potts did not approve of the world in which he found himself, but had, if we are to make any sense of what he said and did, come to believe in the utter foolishness of his hoping to change it for the better. Not only that, but he seemed to think that the hope of changing it for the better supposes that he was a very important man, which he certainly knew he was not. He was neither powerful nor important, and that's that. And to say, as some might, that we are all important in the eyes of God and that therefore Mr Potts is important too, is for him nothing less than a lot of eyewash. I distinctly remember him asserting, quite dismissively, 'A benevolent God makes good men in His own image, and bad men make a malevolent God in theirs, and that's that!' Anyway, Mr Potts began to feel, and continued to feel, that his past hopes for a better world, which really meant hopes for his changing people for the better, was nothing less than impertinent – as though he thought he was something of a saviour when he was not, or as though he thought he knew exactly what would make the world a better place and what would make people better than they are, when he didn't know such things at all. Mr Potts didn't want to say that he was better than the next man, and he didn't even want to *think* it, and he seemed to arrive at the conclusion that the best way to stop thinking such things was to give up thinking altogether! To use another big word, he believed he was being pretentious to set himself up as judge and jury over the whole human race. The way he put it to me was that it's like having been invited to a party (I mean a party to which you have not invited yourself, that is, gate-crashed!) and then criticising the food and the guests and the music and ... Well, I mean, it's not on. The best thing to do would be to put up with the food, the guests and the music and wait things out – for even the worst parties don't go on forever.

And that's what he said he was doing – waiting things out. Yes, he was very angry with the present state of the world, and it wouldn't have taken much to get him making angry speeches about it again, even if it meant him addressing imaginary dignitaries and wise folk in his long bedroom mirror. But, eventually, after anger came grim and silent acceptance – except, of course, for those imaginary excursions into the past, like his recent address to the Senate of ancient Rome, which give him an opportunity to vent his anger concerning events long gone and therefore irreparable. His attention has been turned, you might say, from the present to the past, which is a very natural transition, because what the present and the past have in common, according to Mr Potts, is that nothing at all can be done about either. I hope I have made myself sufficiently obscure. Perhaps a little less obscure is the thought that Mr Potts' interest in the past was connected to his conviction that what happened in the past had created the templates for future human development – and Mr Potts wanted to change, remake, modify and, most importantly, *disarm* the templates created in the past so that the future could stand a better chance. Well, I'm guessing, of course!

Suffice to say, Mr Potts had turned his back on the present, not because he couldn't care a jot about it, but precisely because he cared too much. In this he was rather like the fellow who said he hated all music and was not referring simply to junk music but included the most beautiful works ever written. He loved the beauty of music so much and was so moved by it that he found it too painful to listen to. Well, beauty can pain the eyes of the beholder to such an extent that he has to turn to it a blind eye – the eye that sees too much, blinks and closes. And I am quite sure that the Elves in their great wisdom came to understand that Mr Potts was a creature of the most remarkable sensitivities. They could never bring themselves to ignore a creature of such infinite and rare depths.

But my narrative moves too quickly!

Mr Potts fuelled these excursions into the past by reading a lot. He devoured history books, which does not mean of course that he actually *ate* them, for history books would be very difficult to digest. It means that he just couldn't get enough of them. Any history would do – recent, past, very past, ancient. He'd have even read prehistory if there were any. And it didn't matter which part of the world the history related to. 'It's all the same,' he told me. 'What you find in one place you will find in another, at the same time or a different time. Yes, all the same.' If that's strictly true, one wonders why he didn't simply read the same history book over and over again. But of course it isn't strictly true.

He had a particular interest in ancient Rome and Greece – but especially Rome, since he believed the Romans to have been free of some of the diseases that plague the present. And this I suppose would explain why he dared to hope, in retrospect of course, for better outcomes for Rome, and why he wanted to address the Roman Senate. But I can't help feeling, though I wouldn't have told him as much, that had he actually been able to address the Senate he would soon have found himself entertaining the

Roman mobs in the gladiatorial ring, by taking his last breaths in the mouth of a lion or being cut to pieces by the gladiatorial equivalent of a football icon. Some things are best left unsaid. True, Lucius Annaeus Seneca the Younger, the Roman Stoic philosopher and statesman, might well have given Mr Potts a favourable hearing. Seneca's comment that the gladiatorial amphitheatre was a place where 'all niceties were put aside and it was pure and simple murder' would have appealed to Mr Potts. Seneca was certainly very wise – but, then, look what happened to him! Come to that, look what happens to most wise men. Wisdom carries the highest possible price tag in an unwise world.

Chapter Five

TOUCHING SENSITIVITY

I remember it was one of those chilly but sunny mornings in early autumn when, as was my custom, I called in to see my friend Mr Potts to share a pot of tea and a slice or two of toast. I made a point of appearing once or twice a week, for, after all, I'm the only visitor he had. I found him sitting at the breakfast table pouring a cup of tea and staring at the ceiling at the same time – a hazardous practice but rather typical of Mr Potts when in musing mood, a mood in which he was commonly to be found.

'They don't like it,' he said, as I sat down beside him. I asked him *who* didn't like *what*. '*Who*? The Elves of course! No, they don't like it one little bit!' And *what*? 'Books! – they say there's too many of them, far too many bad ones anyway, especially when everybody decides to write one and actually manages to persuade a publisher to bring it out!' Mr Potts was clearly rattled. The Elves had been lecturing him again, or perhaps he'd just overheard them chatting amongst themselves in one of his dreams.

Now I've said that Mr Potts read a lot. But he detested fiction. He believed, wrongly I think, that if you want to know about people you've got to stick to factual stuff, like history books. I disagree. A good novel is good precisely because it does tell you about people – how they live and think and what makes them tick. I did try, once, to make the point, but he ended up pooh-poohing it, saying that he didn't really object to *good* novels but that there are so few of them that it's hardly worth the effort to try to find them. Anyway, it turned out that morning in early autumn that he had visited a bookshop the day before, looking for yet another book on the history of ancient Rome to add to his already impressive collection, and had felt physically sick at the sight of so many books which, according to him, shouldn't have been allowed to see the light of day – mainly romances, unimaginative thrillers which thrill without substance, autobiographies written by people hardly out of their teens or by sporting icons hell-bent on milking every drop of attention, and books for children, very much in vogue and written by celebrity authors but which, according to Mr Potts, entirely misrepresent the lives and doings of Elves. No doubt the Elves saw with an equal measure of disgust what Mr Potts saw, which gave them a subject to complain about in his dream.

Perhaps at this point I should hazard another big word, but one which Mr Potts once used so frequently and with so much passion that you might be forgiven for thinking that he had invented it himself. The word is 'mediocrity'. The thought once occurred to me that I might, on an occasion when his feathers were well and truly up, actually count the number of times he used the word. Anyway, he said there was too much of it – mediocrity, I mean. He didn't seem to want to abolish it altogether. No, he just wanted it to be rather less, and he wanted it to be put in its rightful place, that's all. He objected most of all to the fact that mediocrity pretends to be something it's not – rather like an ignorant man pretending to be knowledgeable, or a Fiery Dragon pretending to be an Elf, because nasty dragons and Elves are very different, as any little child will tell you. It's not just the pretence in itself but the fact that the pretence is not only allowed but very much encouraged. And when this happens, 'It's like weeds covering up beautiful flowers and hiding them from sight,' said Mr Potts. And that's bad, almost as bad as the murders that took place in the gladiatorial ring – because they were meant to make the mobs happy. Mediocrity, on the scale Mr Potts thought it exists, murders beauty. Beautiful flowers must be given a chance to grow and to be seen. Too many weeds smother them. A garden may be so choked with weeds that people will never get to see the flowers at all! Oh, yes, he used to go on and on about it. If mediocrity had been a living creature, Mr Potts would have battered it to death, hanged, drawn and quartered it and dumped its poor remains into the deepest and murkiest part of the ocean – and I say this knowing full well that Mr Potts was the gentlest creature on God's earth.

I think this is what worried Mr Potts most – I mean the way true beauty is ignored or smothered and is never allowed to see the true light of day, so that for the majority of humans it remains hidden or obscured, even though they have every right to see it, enjoy it and even contribute to it. It worried him to such an extent that in the end he felt it necessary to give up worrying at all, as I have already explained. He could see no solution to the problem of a burgeoning mediocrity, and there came a point where he gave up using the word at all, but, after all, the poor word was most deserving of a long holiday and is now resting somewhere in books called dictionaries and receives fewer and fewer visitors as the years roll by. You might say that the word has adopted the life of an extremely disgruntled recluse, imitating the life of its erstwhile principal user, Mr Potts himself.

Yes, Mr Potts gave up worrying. After all, there is a limit to worrying, because worrying is weakening and, to use another big word just for the sheer fun of it, 'debilitating'. You can worry so much that you begin to feel hollow inside. You begin to feel neglected and, worst of all, irrelevant. Neglected and irrelevant is exactly how the Elves feel, according to Mr Potts. 'No wonder,' he said, 'they keep very much to themselves, inhabit trees and not houses, and appear only to very few humans, and even then only in their sleeping hours in the dead of night'. They obviously made an exception for Mr Potts by making their language comprehensible to him, though it was a language he couldn't reciprocate. He tried to explain this to me, but I was, and still am, at a loss to understand it. I mean, how can it be that he could understand what the Elves said and yet was unable to speak their language? You might as well say that he could and could not speak the language. Absurd! It would make just as much sense to say, 'I understand every word spoken to me in French, but I can't speak a word of it' – and I am assuming that there is nothing at all wrong physically with your mouth or your vocal chords. No, it seems quite contradictory to me. But, once again, I had no alternative but to defer to Mr Potts's superior intellect and agree that some contradictions are well worth considering, as though they are paradoxes and need to be thought about very carefully. Even so, there were many occasions when I couldn't for the life of me understand what Mr Potts was getting at, assuming that he was getting at something at all.

Now it strikes me that the word 'understand' is not a word that people think about very much. I might even say that they don't *understand* it very well. Mr Potts's neighbours thought he was eccentric, even a little mad, even plain bonkers. Maybe that's because they didn't understand him, or didn't understand him well enough. Perhaps they didn't understand where he was coming from – and I don't mean that they didn't know which part of the country he was born in, which would be ridiculous or at least irrelevant. No, I mean they didn't understand why he was so upset about the world in which he found himself. Why, for example, all this ranting and raving about something called 'mediocrity'? What was it all about?

But I suppose we have to say that people are different. If Mr Potts had slipped on a banana skin, some people, I think the vast majority, would have laughed their heads off (not literally, of course). There are some who would have just smiled. But there are others, perhaps the smallest minority, who wouldn't have laughed at all and would even have felt sorry for him and rushed to help him up, asking if he was alright and checking to see if he'd broken any bones.

People are different, and I suppose these are differences we must learn to live with. But maybe some of us find it hard, if not impossible, to live with these differences or to live with them comfortably. I believe, though of course I may be wrong, that Mr Potts was one of those people who just find it impossible to live comfortably with such differences. These differences can't be resolved despite all the worrying and head scratching in the world. But you can scratch your head so much that you grow permanently bald. This, in a manner of speaking, is what happened to Mr Potts – he'd become permanently bald, on the *inside* at least, if you know what I mean.

After all, there are far more important things in life than slipping on banana skins. There are things like wars and mindless cruelties and inhumanities – things which some people just can't live with.

To use another big word, I think it boils down to *sensitivity*. Some people, not many I agree, would go out of their way to avoid stepping on an ant, while others, too many to count I'm afraid, wouldn't think twice about killing you for the few coins in your pocket.

In a phrase, Mr Potts was highly sensitive. But I believe that this was just the thing that made him so attractive to the Elves. One thing they love is sensitivity. They can't get enough of it. But they don't see enough of it amongst us humans. So when they come across someone as sensitive as Mr Potts they embrace him – I mean they accept and even love him – they wouldn't literally embrace him because that would mean physical contact and they would never contact a human physically, as I hope I've already made plain.

Well, this business of differences and sensitivity would help to explain why some people, perhaps most, decided to call my friend Mr Potty Potts, with or without the 'Mr', while some others, a minority no doubt, were respectful enough simply to call him Mr Potts. The difference is between naughty children who would point and laugh at an elderly person who loses his balance, and well behaved and well brought up children who might be expected not to. I say 'might be expected' because even children who have been brought up properly sometimes act badly, and we are all aware of the expression 'boys will be boys' – which means, that we are often faced with the unexpected even when children are brought up nicely.

So there we are. It was, I sincerely believe, on account of Mr Potts's sensitivity that the Elves had decided to make him an exception, to single him out for their especial and caring attention. I've said that they spoke in a language that he could understand, even if they didn't speak *to* him directly. That's very thoughtful of them – which brings us to the very question of language and words, a matter that was very close to Mr Potts's heart. He told me he read a lot, not only to know about things and people of the past, but also to improve his vocabulary and grammar. Someone might say of him that he liked to kill two birds with one stone. But he wouldn't have said this himself, I suppose because he didn't relish the thought of killing anything at all, least of all birds – except of course mediocrity, which, in his opinion, had grown grotesquely obese.

(We all know that 'killing two birds with one stone' doesn't really mean killing two birds with one stone, or killing anything with anything. We know that it only means doing two things at the same time or in the same act. Even so, Mr Potts wouldn't have liked the expression, which is further proof, I think, of his amazing sensitivity.)

Mr Potts chose his books carefully, taking the quality of the writing into account. 'Choose only the best books,' he always said, whereby 'best' I took him to mean the variety of words (vocabulary) and the grammar, as well as the contents. He attached great importance to language, not just *his* language, but *any and every* language. He said you have to take great care of language to prevent it becoming ill. Yes, he spoke of language as though it were a pet cat or dog, because he said it should be fed the best food and taken to the vet whenever it sneezes or coughs – I think he meant dictionary or grammar books when he says 'vet', because he was very careful to check his spelling and his grammar whenever there was the least doubt. 'It's all we've got to separate us from jungle animals,' he once remarked, 'If we allow it to become diseased, it'll be sloppy and floppy and useless and fade away – and then we'll be in a far greater mess than we're in already. The Elves are very conscious of this fact and they attribute some of the mess we're in to this kind of neglect. Well, some things have to be taken very seriously – and language is one of them!' On another occasion he said that the Elves are very careful to give their children the very best examples of the use of language to follow. He was very keen that we should follow suit. On one occasion he jumped up from the breakfast table shouting, 'It leaves nothing out! Nothing at all!' And, noticing my shocked countenance, went on, 'Language. I mean *language*! When you know a language well enough, you know the people who speak it, their hopes, fears, their violence and their affection, their accomplishments and their failures, their strengths and their weaknesses, their deficiencies and their excesses, their dreams and their illusions, what moves them and what stops them in their tracks – everything! Language leaves nothing out. Someone once said that language leaves out things that can't be said, but you must at least be *able to say* what these things *are*! No, I say again, language leaves nothing out! And that's why we've got to try to get it right. Language is a key to understanding, and if a key isn't shaped right it won't turn in the lock!' He sat down again with a tired but satisfied expression on his poor, lined face, as though he had picked up a strange object and had begun to uncover its secrets.I barely understood him, and still don't – not even enough to challenge him, so I let it pass, as I let most things pass. I suppose he meant something, or *wanted* to mean something.

(When he said we should 'follow suit', he didn't of course mean that we should follow a jacket and a pair of trousers, for then we would have said '*a* suit', which is very silly – he just meant that we should do the same things as the Elves do, and give our children the very best examples to follow.)

Of course, people who called him Potty Potts would say that he was going over the top with all this emphasis on the best examples. They would say it doesn't really matter because there's no right or wrong way of doing things. But Mr Potts would have strongly disagreed. He said, 'If anything goes, nothing goes.' He was a stickler for rules and standards. He expected the best, or did once upon a time. The time came, of course, when he expected nothing at all, except the very best from himself.

Having said that, though Mr Potts was far from being a simpleton, despite what some people mockingly called him ('Simple Simon', though his first name was Edward!), he did enjoy the simple things in life, such as tea and toast for breakfast, indeed *especially* tea and toast, or any simple meal when hungry, such as sausage and mash, and a cup of tea when relaxing, 40 winks when he felt sleepy, the singing of birds in the early morning, the pitter-patter of rain on the windows when he was warm and dry inside, the aroma of wild flowers and undergrowth when he was out walking – and I believe I can count the little morning chats we used to have once or twice a week (three times in the winter). I say 'chats', but he never really did say very much, I mean not in any lengthy or connected way – not like the speech he made to the Senate, but rather in dribs and drabs. It would be better to say that he tended to 'come out' with things – by which I don't mean that he emptied his pockets or anything like that, but only that he said things now and again without explaining what had gone before or giving an inkling of what should come after, leaving things in mid-air, so to speak. In fact, everything I know, or believe I know, about Mr Potts is a result of his 'coming out with things' quite unexpectedly and in disconnected ways.

Anyway, as I say, he was a simple man with simple needs and was easily satisfied with simple things. His interest in history in general and his attachment to ancient Rome in particular were serious hobbies, not quite obsessions. They were in any case his only interests – everything else was a matter of simple routine. His preference for the simple things in life came about, I think, when he came to see that it is quite useless to worry yourself sick about the state of the world and the people in it, because these are things which you can do little about, especially when it comes to *homo homini lupus* – little, that is, apart from setting the best example you can, because talking seems useless and force is counter-productive (a big word, I know, but I am stuck for a simpler one, no doubt because I lack Mr Potts's wonderfully varied store of vocabulary).

Mr Potts's lifestyle may have been simplicity itself. But he had certainly been through the hoop (by this I don't mean that he physically jumped through big rings made of wood or plastic – I just mean that he had some very painful experiences).

It was one of those tea and toast mornings when, spreading some butter on a slice of toast with the tip of a carving knife, he suddenly said, 'When my angel ascended ...' he paused as if to ensure that every bit of toast was covered. 'Y'know, they write songs of love and of loss. But there was no music when she died – only a grim, empty, cold sort of silence.' I guess I knew, instinctively, that he was referring to his wife, partly because it was the kind of way he sometimes spoke and partly because on this occasion his eyes seemed to well up with tears. 'When my angel ascended, the last door was locked tight against me and no door would open again. The reason for taking the next breath went with her. I saw everything in 3D. Disease, Decline and Death!' – which, by the way, is just how the Elves see our lives, according to Mr Potts, and so it's no wonder that they thank their lucky stars they aren't human and don't do as humans do. In the old days, he said, they used to sing songs round their midnight campfires deep in the forest about the good things humans do, but, over the centuries, the good things have been so overshadowed by the bad that they gave up singing and have taken to having early nights instead.

Well, that was that. He offered me the toast he had buttered, and I knew that if and when he said anything else, the subject would be very different. By this time in our relationship I had learned to restrain myself whenever he came out with something that was clearly very deeply personal. But little by little my knowledge of Mr Potts was taking shape by osmosis – you know, when blots of ink expand on blotting paper and form shapes you think you might recognise.

Chapter Six

A FAILED EXPEDITION

I've already pointed out that Mr Potts was a man of very few words and that his sentences were like pieces of a jigsaw puzzle handed out one by one, I mean a piece at a time, and that the picture was almost always left incomplete.

There were times, though, when, to use another big word, he became quite *loquacious* – I mean, he spoke a lot, or at least far more than usual, even if he still left things incomplete and never quite finished what he'd started.

One such memorable occasion was a Christmas Eve. Mr Potts had given up using central heating a long time before that and preferred his log fire, using the dead wood he'd collected all year round and stored under a large sheet of tarpaulin at the bottom of the garden. One thing he would not do. He refused to chop bits of branches off live trees to store up for the winter.

He said trees are living creatures that naturally take offence to humans lopping off their tentacles for their own thoughtless ends. Instead, he collected any dead bits of wood he found on his walks, unless he could see that they had already become homes for insects and worms and such things, because to make such creatures homeless is also something he refused point blank to do. It hardly needs to be said that the care he took and the consideration he showed was something carefully observed and commented upon very favourably by the Elves. For there is nothing that sickens an Elf more than the sight of mindless pillage – according to Mr Potts.

Anyway, there's something special about a real fire in the living room at Christmas time, especially when the room is in darkness, save for the red glow of the embers and the darting flames that make shadows on the walls. There must be, because the effect it had on Mr Potts is worth noting.

It was while we were sitting together on that Christmas Eve watching the fire while the shadows danced behind and around us that he began to tell me of the time, it must have been after his angel had ascended (to put it as Mr Potts might have put it), that he decided to pack a bag with essentials and get away from it all, leaving his house and all the things in it, and perhaps never ever coming back. He packed two bottles of drinking water, some dried food, some clean underclothes and a clean shirt, a notebook and pen, one of his favourite books (*A Brief History of Rome*), his pipe, tobacco and matches, a miniature oil stove, together with a slim sleeping bag and a small tent. When he looked at the bulging bag he wondered how he would struggle with it to the garden gate, let alone through the undergrowth of forests and down country lanes. Putting such thoughts to the back of his mind, he set out early one morning in spring. When he reached the garden gate he had what he described to me as a stroke of genius – he would catch a train, just to get him on his way, far from the madding crowd, and then his back-packing could begin in earnest. This was done, and after two hours or so in a stuffy train compartment he alighted on a lonely platform somewhere well away from the hustle and bustle of the town.

Once out of the railway station, he set off down leafy lanes, and across fields with signs pinned to gates warning trespassers that they would be prosecuted if caught. Mr Potts found it quite thrilling to be visibly and defiantly on the wrong side of the law for a change. But he was always glad to pitch tent and sleep under the stars, even if the tent did let in the rain, which it did almost every night. His water and dried provisions soon ran out and the whole prospect of spending the rest of his life learning how to fish without a rod and line or how to set traps for rabbits without actually causing them any harm at all did not appeal to him in the slightest. In short, he spent a very miserable week inside a very wet tent, with the raindrops pitter-pattering onto the pages of his *A Brief History of Rome* as he tried to distract himself from the foul weather and a very mistaken decision.

It is testimony to the sharpness of his intellect that he lost little time in reaching the conclusion that a life of wandering and of sleeping under the stars was really not for him. He could not live like the Elves and spent many a happy hour wondering how on earth they managed to live in trees and sleep under carpets of leaves. How could they possibly do it and him not? Once again, his unique intellect came up with the answer: quite simply, he was *very probably not* an Elf! (I purposely stress the phrase 'very probably not'.) After a week of rain-soaked misery, he was forced to abandon the life of a hermit. A house of stone had a great deal to say for it over a wet, chilly tent. And so, he was fated to suffer the proximity of his fellow men. He was clearly reminded of his fate as he struggled up the garden path on his return. He sensed some of the neighbours watching him through their curtains and imagined them chuckling at the sight of a very damp, bedraggled and dishevelled Potts puffing and panting towards his front door with a bulging bag on his back like some aging street seller or hawker of old trying to sell his poor wares in an unfriendly metropolis and expecting nothing but a curse and a blow for all his pains. It was considered further and damning proof, if any were needed, of the Potty nature of Mr Potts. It's very odd how the strongest of conclusions may frequently be drawn from the weakest of premises.

Well, at least he could close his door upon the world outside and choose his friends carefully, though I am still at a loss why he should have chosen me. And for company he had the Elves, who were always laughing their little green socks off at the antics and misdeeds of humans – even when humans are very bad to each other, in fact especially then, because the lives of humans are already quite short and full of problems, and yet they behave towards one another as though they should do everything in their power to make life even shorter and as miserable as possible. Just think of the horrible weapons humans devise, and continually strive to 'improve', to rid themselves of one another! Mr Potts said that such nonsense makes the Elves laugh, though, as you may well suspect, their laughter is spiced with morbid wonder and not a little grief. According to Mr Potts, human life seems to the Elves both a tragedy and a comedy, both at one and the same time, which seems to them illogical. If we believe Mr Potts, and I see no good reason why we shouldn't, the average Elf can't decide whether the life of humans is a tragedy or a comedy, or more or less of the one than the other – well, apparently, they resolve the whole thing by laughing their heads off and frequently losing their little green hats in the process.

(Of course, when Mr Potts said they laugh their heads off, he didn't really mean that their heads fall off, because then, since they have so much to laugh about, there wouldn't be any Elf left! They would all become headless in the first flush of laughter. No, he just meant that they laugh very loudly and shake a lot – or something like that.)

So there we are. There was no escape for Mr Potts from the lunacy of his fellow humans – though it has to be said that he frequently doubted whether he himself *was* human, and he confided in me sufficiently to tell me so. But he didn't know for sure that he *wasn't* an Elf – he just wasn't sure that he *was*! He couldn't speak their language, despite the fact that they allowed him to understand what they were telling each other, and that uncomfortable week under a wet tent was, he said, at least *evidence* that he wasn't one of them, though he was quick to add that evidence, however strong, does not amount to definitive proof! I myself believe that Mr Potts was definitely human – one thing that clinches it was his love of tea and toast. Somehow I can't imagine an Elf tucking in to tea and toast at a kitchen table or any other sort of table – although for Elves anything is possible, as long as it isn't *in*human, of course!

But no, there is one thing that, above all others, separated Mr Potts from the Elves he so admired. And that was his inability to laugh at the stupidity of his fellow humans. For Mr Potts, there could have been no comedy about the tragic stupidity of man's inhumanity to man. While the Elves have difficulty deciding whether human behaviour is comic or tragic, Mr Potts had made up his mind long ago. He couldn't even work up a smile over it, let alone laugh his head off. No, it was a constant thorn in his side.

(When I say 'thorn', I don't really mean that he's brushed up against a rose bush and picked up a splinter. I just mean that he was annoyed, or irritated, or pained.)

'I only laugh when there is something funny to laugh about,' he once remarked, and I thought that was very sensible. But, come to think of it, I never heard Mr Potts laugh at anything at all! Did I ever see him even smile? No, I don't think so. I hear you ask whether someone without a visible sense of humour could possibly be so amazingly intelligent as to border on sheer genius, like Mr Potts, and I do agree that it's very puzzling.

Perhaps he laughed when I wasn't around. Perhaps he laughed when he was alone. All I know is that I never heard him laugh and I doubt whether I ever saw him smile, and that's that! He was really quite expressionless, and so, unless you came to know him as I did, you wouldn't be quite sure what he was thinking. Of course, I can't say exactly what he was thinking at any particular time, but I do know that it wasn't going to be something that might break him out in a laugh at any moment – so he wouldn't be thinking of making a joke about something, for example. Mr Potts was no entertainer. What's more, he refused to be entertained. When I first became acquainted with him I was struck by his quiet ways and serious expression and I thought I'd cheer him up with a funny story – well, he listened patiently enough, but he didn't laugh when the funny bit came at the end, so I gave up trying to be humorous. No, you might just as well have expected him to stand on his head than to laugh. Anyway, I couldn't read his mind, but I knew that his thoughts were nothing to laugh at.

(When I say 'I couldn't read his mind', I don't mean that a mind is a book, leaflet or newspaper – some small volume hidden inside a head with pages with words written on them. I mean, I couldn't have told you what he was thinking.)

Mr Potts told me once that when he heard the Elves laughing at the human condition he couldn't understand why they did it, and with such gusto. He expected them to shed tears of pain, not of joy. I said that sometimes things can be so bad that the only thing you can do is laugh. He said that that made as much sense to him as a bottomless boat or a wingless bird. After a while, I had to agree with him. I confess, I have never ever seen a bottomless boat unless it's a wreck and so no longer a boat. Neither have I seen a wingless bird, unless it's chopped up ready for the oven and so no longer a bird. But there are those who would disagree and say that a bottomless boat is still a boat, a wingless bird still a bird. Well, when you can't resolve something like this, perhaps the best thing is to laugh. Mr Potts would disagree. I think he would say the best thing is to keep quiet. After all, he lived his life according to the saying 'Silence is golden'.

(Incidentally, this doesn't mean that silence really *is* golden. You might as well say that silence is oblong or square or stands on four shaky legs. Silence isn't anything of the sort. It just means that silence is sometimes a very good idea. Many sayings are like this – they don't mean what they seem to mean, rather like the people who make them up.)

Chapter Seven

CONTENTMENT

After his failed attempt to live the life of a wandering hermit, Mr Potts was obliged to settle down in his little house, cosy and warm, and isolated as far as possible from the world outside, as though the world of humans was an unwanted Christmas present that couldn't even be given away and was buried in a drawer under a pile of old clothes and to all intents and purposes forgotten. Mr Potts wrapped himself in the warm blanket of memories of events and loved ones long gone, so that it may be said with some gravity and not a little regret that he formed a closer relationship with the dead than he felt could ever be possible with the living. He sacrificed the present for the past and attempted to conceal the pitiful transaction in a myriad of trivial, routine activities about the house and garden, as though the current affairs of humans were taking place in someone else's dream – or, rather, *nightmare*.

Given his contempt for the doings of humans, it's no surprise that his television set failed to secure a lasting place in his affections. Programmes which feature chats with celebrities only made him ill, because they are, he complained, no more than celebrations of mediocrity, and, when celebrities appear together, it's always a kind of mutual admiration society, a kind of exchange of self-advertising, all those concerned being intoxicated by their own self-esteem – or so he said. As for general knowledge quizzes, he insisted that people shouldn't be called clever just because they know a lot. In the first place, *what* they know, he insisted, is seldom important, and, in the second place, knowing something is not at all the same as the ability to think and reach conclusions – knowing is not the same as intellect, being knowledgeable is not the same as being clever, so that an ignorant person may nevertheless be extremely clever, and a knowledgeable person may be quite stupid! He said that if you read a book about, say, life in Roman Britain, you can reasonably claim to know more than you did before, to be more knowledgeable than you were before, but you cannot reasonably claim to be cleverer than you were before. He insisted that cleverness, like genius, was a *capacity*, and one that is 'a given' – it can be practised and it can be honed, it can be utilised or it can be ignored, it can be latent or it can be obvious, but it can't be *created*. Anyway, that's what he claimed, and I was in no better position than I am now to say whether or not what he claimed to be true is in fact true. But, as on so many other occasions, what Mr Potts said prompted me to ask questions on matters which I had taken very much for granted. In fact, he once said that it's more important to ask the right questions than to provide answers to wrong questions – the ability to ask the right questions was, he said, a true mark of cleverness. People ask questions to which they then seek answers, but Mr Potts said that they should take on board Plato's advice about prayers and apply it to the questions they ask, namely that we should first pray that we have the right desires before we pray that our desires be fulfilled!

Further evidence of Mr Potts's own intellect, of his ability to think and draw conclusions, was his decision to dispose of his television set by dropping it unceremoniously into a big hole which he had dug for the very purpose at the bottom of his garden. After filling the hole in, he planted a rough crucifix upon it bearing the words *Requiescat in Pace* ('Rest in Peace', or, more precisely, 'May he/she Rest in Peace', he was at pains to point out). He believed that television has outlived its usefulness and has become little more than a purveyor of mindless violence and bloodlust masquerading as good entertainment, especially during the Season of Goodwill to All Men, namely Christmas.

This was explained to me in typical staccato and unfinished sentences when I noticed the crucifix through his kitchen window and inquired about it. He had a preference for Latin phrases and tags, which I thought a bit pedantic until I got to know him better. But no doubt it came from his deep interest in ancient Rome. I can confidently say that it didn't have anything to do with the *Church* of Rome – or for that matter any other

Church. Mr Potts was not what I would call a religious man in any orthodox sense. Mind you, I never questioned him about religion, nor would I even have dared to. If he had had by any chance much to say on the matter I would have risked being 'staccato-ed' to death, as it were, in the telling, needing the much vaunted patience of Job to bear it. No, like many other things concerning Mr Potts, I would much prefer to infer for myself, based on my own observations, than to be told, even if I don't get it quite right. What can possibly be worse than a very long account of a person's religious beliefs, or lack of them, which leaves you really no wiser and totally flushed with irritation? – it would be like peeling a gigantic onion only to see it restored again at the end of it all, a very tearful process and entirely in vain.

(You will readily understand that when I say 'gigantic onion' I am not referring to a real onion that happens also to be very large. I have nothing at all against onions, large or small, but I am using the phrase 'gigantic onion' figuratively to refer to something complicated, something with different *layers*, just as an onion has layers. Moreover, peeling onions makes you cry, and Mr Potts may well have had the same effect on you should he have attempted an explanation long and complex.)

In the first place, I never heard him say anything about religion, *any* religion, and I never heard him use any turn of phrase or utter any word which could have been said to have religious significance, either figurative or literal. True, and as I have already explained, Mr Potts rarely did go on at length to me about any subject at all. But, as I hope I have also explained, he had the astonishing ability to pack a great deal of meaning into very few words– he was, and here I borrow from him one of his favourite Latin tags, a man of very few words, *par excellence*. (The Latin refers to an instance of a thing which is a very good example of that kind of thing.) In this he reminded me of what I myself have read of the average (if there is such a thing) spiritual leader amongst the Native Americans of old – namely that they said very little at all when conducting their religious ceremonies, in stark contrast to their white counterparts who say too much and typically so much that they bore their congregations into states of somnolence at a depth that renders them entirely inaccessible to the Holy Spirit. But now I digress.

Given that the language of religion was entirely absent from Mr Potts's vocabulary, and because of the fact that Mr Potts made no reference whatsoever to anything that could possibly be construed as an appeal to Scripture, and, given his distaste for humans and his fervent wish that he had been of another and better species, being more than fully aware of his own shortcomings as a human, and, given his contempt for dishonesty, selfishness, cruelty, inhumanity and deception, and given his abandonment of hope for the improvement of the human condition and his desire to isolate himself from the entire world of human affairs, it may well be inferred that the contempt he felt in the generality is easily applied to organised religions in the particular, since these feature in the doings of humans and have themselves repeatedly been and still are the cause of much dissension and mutual contempt, not say loathing, not to say armed conflict!

I must say that Mr Potts seemed extremely hard done by, by nature or fortune or a toxic mixture of the two. For, after all, religion of whatever sort seems to function as a balm for believers. Religion is meant to soothe the mind and offer consolation and comfort to all those who despair of man and seek to place their hopes elsewhere. It is something to which believers may appeal in moments of doubt or stress, a support, one might say, as they traverse the winding, twisting, hostile byways of life, and it is a definite source of courage when life is at its ebb and eternal darkness beckons. Alas, alack, Mr Potts saw nothing in religion but a source of endless trouble and strife – perhaps because he believed humans are not sufficiently capable of understanding correctly and not good enough to follow the religions in which they profess to believe. Perhaps he believed that there can be no such thing as a *good* religion, because it is in the nature of all religions that they will defeat themselves with their lack of clarity, their tendency to mislead and, so often, their lack of simple humanity, or their lack of soul – ironically, since the word 'soul' looms large in their lexicon. Anyway, religion was out as far as Mr Potts was concerned. He preferred to measure people by what they do rather than by what they say, because what they say is almost always muddled when it comes to something like religion. Everyone would agree that it's useless, sometimes very dangerous, to speak about things you don't know. Religion is something that nobody really understands very well, and yet it's amazing how much people talk about it, often referring to what has been written in Scripture as though the written word is by itself sufficient to validate without question what is said even when what is said makes little or no sense at all, or when the sense it makes is entirely misunderstood. Scripture is called 'Holy', which means for most of its followers that you can't *question* it, and for many it means that you can't even discuss it but only recite it and commit it to memory, as though memorising it *validates* it! – and as though uttering words and memorising them will make you *a better person*. The mind boggles. No wonder Mr Potts was sickened by the whole thing if these were his thoughts! I must agree with him – humans are indeed difficult cases.

But this is me theorising beyond my licence, because, as I said, I didn't approach my friend Mr Potts on this subject, and I wouldn't have dared to – I think partly because it would have rekindled in him the anger and frustration that he had managed to free himself from by having nothing more to do with the world of humans. But, as we are forming a generalised portrait of Mr Potts, it seems only fair to have mentioned that he was not what most people would consider of a religious turn of mind.

Imagine then my shock, not to say alarm, when, during one of our regular tea and toast sessions, he suddenly exclaimed, arms and hands outstretched towards the ceiling, 'Blessed! Blessed be the Lord God for giving comfort to us poor mortals!' after which, and without further ado, he poured himself a cup of tea and took a preliminary chunk out of his first piece of toast with considerable relish, as if to signal that the subject was closed as quickly as it was opened. My first thought was that he had given vent to his distaste for religion with an ironic or a sarcastic exclamation. But there was no hint of either irony or sarcasm, not so much as a single smirk or a solitary 'Humph!' His exclamation had been delivered with Pentecostal enthusiasm and therefore had to go unchallenged.

(I use the word 'irony', which, though it has a metallic ring to it, has nothing to do with iron, nor indeed with ironing. In fact, it's a very difficult notion to explain, partly because it's a house of many mansions, which means that it's of very different kinds – just in case you're wondering whether I'm talking about a real house of bricks and mortar. The word 'irony' can mean almost anything you want it to mean, because life is full of oddities and inconsistencies, of things which are not what they are said to be. To use an example which would be very close to Mr Potts's heart, Cicero, a Roman writer, said that the Romans brought destruction and called it peace. And it does seem odd to destroy things in the name of peace. Then there are people who take pleasure in hurting you, yet profess at the same time to love you. Very odd, not to say wicked. Life is full of such irony – the world staggers under its weight! Anyway, I digress.)

The irony that comes to mind when I think of Mr Potts is that his isolation was a kind of consolation. In other words, it is an inescapable fact of life that the more you love someone the more you are hurt when they leave you, not to mention when they die and leave you forever. There is no love without grief, it seems, and the more you love, the more you grieve when the person you love dies – and die we all must, for only the Elves are exempt from man's mortal coil. But this is not irony, or at least not the irony I mean. The irony I mean is that Mr Potts's isolation shielded him from the misery of *loss,* but at the expense of the misery of *loneliness.* He consoled himself in his isolation, since he had no friends, with the thought that he couldn't be hurt when they passed on. Well, I do agree, it's a poor consolation. But the further irony is that despite Mr Potts's distaste for all organised religions, he seems to have had at least this much in common with Buddhists, with all their talk about un-attachment (or is it *de*tachment, or *dis*attachment?), an idea that probably shields them from an excess of grief, but at the expense of a deficit of passion and of love. The devotees might be content, but I don't quite see how they can be truly happy. In this regard, Mr Potts would have made a good Buddhist – content, perhaps, but not happy.

It might be worth mentioning that although Mr Potts and I got on quite well, and well enough to sit together in his kitchen enjoying tea and toast, I'm pretty sure he wouldn't have grieved long had I shaken off this mortal coil before him. I doubt if I'll be even a nine-day wonder. I am what Mr Potts might have called an 'acquaintance' or even 'close acquaintance', a friendly witness as it were, an amicable companion of sorts. I called him a friend. Perhaps I speak loosely. Anyway, it's not a word he'd have used of me, of that I feel sure. Of course, it's perfectly true that the word 'friend' is used very loosely. As a corrective, someone once said that if you can find even one true friend in life you should count yourself extremely lucky.

Saint Augustine remarked, 'A friend is someone to whom you can reveal the secrets of your heart'. The Saint's idea is well taken, but many would, on reflection, say that the fellow was suffering from a surfeit of expectation – also, you may feel obliged to reveal the secrets of your heart to an analyst and yet not count him your friend, or even to your enemy, under torture or duress. Mr Potts revealed himself to me as it were *en passant* or in an incidental fashion and not in full flushes, so what I was to him remains a foggy matter.

Be that as it may, it was no doubt this business of choosing contentment over happiness that intrigued the Elves and motivated them to get to know him better and visit him in his dreams, if I can speak here of 'choosing'. I mean, it was this, together with his deep interest in the past as distinct from the present – an interest so keen, in fact, that he never went anywhere without a small trowel which he kept in his overcoat pocket, in case he came across a bump in a hill or a small uneven piece of ground which he thought might be worth uncovering – excavating in miniature, of course. Perhaps he imagined he might unearth something new and exciting, like a Roman coca-cola tin or an Anglo Saxon bicycle pump. I jest, of course. I can't resist the odd jibe, not because I wish to belittle him, but because his seriousness seemed to demand a kind of counterweight, which I provided in the form of humour – discreetly, of course, and entirely unbeknown to him. No wonder the Elves found him an intriguing character and more than faintly amusing.

Chapter Eight

SIMPLICITY

Mr Potts was no ordinary historian. He was no ordinary gardener, either. Gardening, it might be said, was his second love – of course we use the word 'love' very loosely. 'Turn your back on it and all hell's let loose,' he once said while looking out of the kitchen window. 'The garden?' I enquired. He nodded. 'Just like human life,' he added with a sigh. From which I felt free to deduce that Mr Potts viewed nature in ways similar to that in which he viewed human beings. This might've explained his desire for perfection and tidiness, which must surely have been second to none – which in turn explains why all his plants, flowers and small shrubs stood together encased in terracotta pots on the stone-slab patio, as though to attention and ready for inspection. Should a leaf or petal have the temerity to fall on his patio, Mr Potts would sweep it up quick as a flash so that all was tidy and in order again, like the lady I was once told of who would suspend a sentence in the middle of a flowing conversation in order to stoop and pick up a crumb from her very clean carpet in her spick and span living room. I suppose he would have said that plants are like humans. Some are very pretty and their sole function seems to be that of being desired for their looks, while others cause nothing but trouble and need to be weeded out, and some others, like roses bereft of all the aroma of roses, are imposters, dressed up to look like the real thing – but, whether good or bad, all are doomed to suffer the same fate, ashes to ashes, dust to dust, dry leaves to dry leaves, and dry leaves to compost.

Mr Potts's attempts to bring order out of horticultural disarray extended also to the lowest branches of the trees that lay at the bottom of his garden. On one of my tea and toast visits, I was surprised to find him hanging almost fully upside down on one of the lower branches of the huge sycamore tree that still stands in the far corner of his garden, fully absorbed in sawing off the lowest branches where they appeared to almost touch the ground. It was a bizarre sight, and my first thought was that he could easily have done the same job from a standing position on the ground. But he later insisted that he could get a better and more precise result by getting above the offending branches. Even so, he lost his balance and fell to the ground, the saw following at speed and giving him a nasty bump on the head. 'You need to control it,' he managed to mutter. By 'it' he meant the tree, not the saw.

I suppose I can sympathise with his comparisons. I mean, very good people, like very nice flowers, can't be expected to grow in barren ground. People aren't born bad. But they aren't born good, either. Beautiful flowers, like good people, need to be nurtured in good, healthy ground. But nothing is guaranteed. Though given the best chances and the best nourishment, some flowers never bloom as they should, and even some weeds put some flowers in the shade.

(When I say 'in the shade', I don't mean in a dark place. I mean that some weeds look better than some flowers.)

As for the Elves, Mr Potts told me that they admired his striving for perfection, order and tidiness, but, he said, they preferred variety, because everything has a function. One thing seems to need its opposite. How could we admire beauty if ugliness didn't exist, or what would goodness mean without the existence of evil? Even so, Mr Potts believed that there is too much of the one and too little of the other, too much ugliness and not enough beauty, too much evil and too little goodness. He therefore continued to demand excessive order, tidiness and perfection as a kind of poor consolation. Well, as for excess, I suppose if you don't aim for the top of a very high mountain, you'll never get even half-way there.

Oh, I almost forgot to mention that Mr Potts placed great emphasis on children, comparing them with delicate seedlings. Children, he insisted, must receive the right nourishment and be brought up in the right soil, otherwise you can't expect much of a yield. But I think he blamed himself for not providing the right kind of soil for his own children, since they hardly ever communicated with him. He once remarked that having children is a mixed blessing. He meant that having children is both a wonderful thing and also something very unpleasant. Now this was something I couldn't possibly let pass without explanation, so I asked him to clarify. He explained, in fits and starts, that loving your children is most right and proper, but that the more you love them the more you fear for them – and amongst your greatest fears is knowing that after your death you will no longer be able to support them through hard times. In fact, this fear is much greater, he insisted, than the fear of your own demise. Well, at least Mr Potts was consistent, since it showed how little faith he placed in the world and its human inhabitants. When you bring children into a world as dark as Mr Potts imagined it to be, you may well feel guilty for having done so and may be forgiven for fearing the worst for those you love most. Anyway, when he said that having children is a mixed blessing, he meant that their very existence is a mixture of joy and pain – the more you love them, the more you fear for them.

I believe it is just this kind of thing that endeared Mr Potts to the Elves, though I also believe that they would have wanted Mr Potts to have a little more faith in the power of goodness. As for the fate which we must all share – well, nothing much can be done about that. Those who make fun of Mr Potts would be hard pressed to understand how his eccentricities and his negativity stem from a superabundance of love.

That superabundance meant that poor Mr Potts would have an unusually lonely and difficult life. *Life?* Well, there were those cruel enough to say that Mr Potts had been dead all his life long – 'What a pity he never found football in the way that some people find God!' Mr Potts would not, of course, have understood such cruel jibes, if only because he could not have understood the kind of heads that they came from, anymore than they could have understood *his.* As for the charge that he had been dead all his life long, I remember I once raised the subject of death and the fear it inspires in almost all of us. He simply said that it is life, not death, that should make us tremble, what with the evils of which humans are capable and which they never tire of amply demonstrating. But I recall him mumbling to himself, 'I've been dead for years, and I can thoroughly recommend it' – a strange remark, one of a kind I had come to expect of him, one which gave me much food for thought at the time and has done ever since, because it's one that would appear to be a possible response to the charge levelled against him by cynical gossipers, a response which, had they heard it, would have puzzled them no end, for he seemed to be happily agreeing, in some sense, with their judgement that he had never really 'lived'! – a word which, I think, requires the inverted commas I give it. And I use the phrase 'in some sense' because what words mean depends very often on the sense we *choose* to give them, and the sense we give them isn't always apparent and is so often easily missed if grasped at all! But there was so much that was puzzling about Mr Potts, and much that remained puzzling in the continuing absence of a clear and clarifying conversation, for such conversations were eccentrically absent in relations with him.

In fact, I couldn't have imagined Mr Potts having a (dare I use the word?) 'normal' conversation with anyone. The closest I heard him come to the usual give-and-take, the common exchanges between people, is when he spoke to the birds – and then, obviously, I only heard half the conversation, I mean *his* contribution. It was when I stood watching him pruning away in the hedgerow. 'I can't help that!' he said. 'Yes, yes, I know that perfectly well. I can assure you I'll do my level best. I can't promise more than that. You can see full well how careful I am. All *you* have to do is look after your own patch.' The only other living thing I could see in the vicinity was a small bird, I think a robin, which was tweeting away with a sense of urgency, possibly afraid that Mr Potts would disturb its nesting place. 'Ouch! Now look what you've made me do. I hope you're satisfied. What? Oh, alright, alright, I know.' And so this extraordinary one-sided conversation (if there can possibly be such a thing) ended with Mr Potts wrapping his finger in a handkerchief, turning round and greeting me with a nonchalant good morning. Of course I pretended to have come on the scene that very instant, having heard nothing that had come before.

Neighbours noticed how he greeted the birds in the morning and how they seem to greet him, which in their minds only served to validate the name they gave him, the one they taught their children because it made the little ones laugh – 'Potty Potts'.

I might mention that Mr Potts's tete-a-tete with birds extended also to insects. When walking through the wooden archway, which leads on to the slab patio, he walked into a cobweb. He brushed the cobweb indignantly from around his face, turned to the spider (which, by the way, I didn't see but assumed to be there) and, standing with legs apart and hands on his hips, like a sergeant major about to tear into a raw recruit, barked, 'Well, I take it you're a newcomer!I walk through here every day – no , *several* times a day. I'm sorry, but this is no place to weave your webs. For goodness sake get your act together and learn from your mistakes!' Mr Potts was in no way inhibited by my presence. In fact, and as always, I felt I was there and was not there, as if in a dream, or as if observing from afar. Yes, as if in a dream. But Mr Potts was real enough.

Yes, *real*. Now it has just occurred to me that I have said little or nothing about Mr Potts's appearance and personal vices. It's only fair that I should correct this omission to help validate my claim that Mr Potts was real and not simply a figment of my weird imagination. But any description of Mr Potts is bound to be disappointing.

The fact of the matter is that the only remarkable thing about Mr Potts's appearance is that it was quite *un*remarkable – if that makes much sense, which I very much doubt. He was rather short and on the stocky side, bearded and in his late 60s, though he still sported a good mop of hair which, unlike his beard, was not over-keen to turn white. He was seldom to be seen without his tweed jacket and matching waistcoat, both of which had seen much better days. I say 'mop' of hair, but he was at pains to keep both it and his beard reasonably short and tidy, a fact that should not surprise you given his attention to order and tidiness on his patio of potted plants. If he could have grown his beard and hair in pots, I have no doubt that he would have done so – so much easier to manage! Oh, I was forgetting his old fedora, which I believe I've already mentioned – he was so attached to it that it seemed glued on.

So, there you have it – a most unremarkable portrait of a very remarkable little man. And yet, this isn't an uncommon contrast. It's the same in the world of work. Very remarkable people may be doing the most unremarkable jobs, and, perhaps even more commonly, the most unremarkable people are charged with the most remarkable tasks and paid very handsomely for it! There may be a lot of 'pick', but very little 'match' in the world of humans.

As for his vices, they were like hen's teeth – few and far between.

(You will no doubt know that this reference to hen's teeth is not meant to suggest that hens have teeth or that they should have teeth or that they are in any way culpable for, or sadly deficient in, not having teeth. On the contrary, the point is precisely that no hen has teeth, so to compare something with hen's teeth is to say that it hardly exists or doesn't exist at all. So, Mr Potts's vices hardly existed or did not exist at all.)

Mr Potts had once heard it said, or perhaps he'd read it in a horoscope, that he would never be happy until he could achieve moderation in all things. Firmly believing that he must curb his strongest desires and avoid any excess, he taught himself to be content with little when it comes to personal indulgences. Therefore, he smoked one pipe of tobacco once a week and only in the summer when he could smoke it outdoors and avoid blackening the interior decor – he called this the 'smoking season'. And when, and only when, he smoked his pipe, he also drank a glass of beer – *one* glass only, mind you! It follows that he drank no more than one glass of beer a week and only in the smoking season. Now can you be more moderate than that? Of course, real smokers and drinkers might well ask why on earth he bothered at all. But Mr Potts was of the opinion that the less frequent a thing is the more special it becomes, and that the more special it becomes the more intensely pleasurable it is. And this is, I must say, a faultless piece of logic, provided, that is, you don't question its premise – and there are quite a few humans who would do precisely that!

So it's understandable that when he smoked his pipe and slowly imbibed his beer, he didn't like to be disturbed. I found this out to my cost when I called upon him unexpectedly one afternoon in summer. He just waved me away with a wave of his hand through the smoke in which his head was enshrouded, and I was obliged to retreat back down the garden path feeling as though I had interrupted a religious or mystical ceremony. Needless to say, thereafter I approached the garden most gingerly during the summer period. But Mr Potts was good enough to explain the whole thing, though he offered no apology for the embarrassment I felt.

He also explained that the Elves also enjoy pipes but draw the line at beer. Beer has a calorific value too high for them, since they need to watch their weight. He mentioned an Elven recipe and said something about 'oak leaves together with' a pinch of this and a pinch of that, all fermented in honey water for at least a year, which they use as a substitute for beer. But the recipe went over my head and I didn't think it worth writing down – something I now regret.

To put all this in a nutshell, Mr Potts strived for simplicity and moderation in all things. In all things, I should hasten to add, except his somewhat excessive emphasis on horticultural order, tidiness and perfection, and on an idea of impeccable moral perfection which he believed the world of humans to be tragically lacking! Yes, he was very excessive when it came to human imperfection, because there was nothing moderate about his criticism of so-called human nature, or about the place of weeds in his spotless potted garden. Well, I suppose it's one of those inconsistencies that made Mr Potts what he was – an eccentric, of sorts, in the eyes of those who saw some good in him, and Potty Potts in the eyes of those who didn't see any. Anyway, who ever said that a man must be judged by perfect consistency in all things? If anyone did say it, they'd be infinitely pottier than Mr Potts himself.

(By the way, when I said 'to put all this in a nutshell', I didn't actually mean a real nutshell. After all, the only thing that should be put into a nutshell is a nut, though it's true that nuts are usually taken out, not put in. What I mean, of course, is 'to be brief'.)

I note with some concern that I have used the word 'simple' quite a lot when talking about Mr Potts and his ways. I should say again and without further ado that very few things are simple. I have often wondered about ideas of simplicity, and the more I have thought about them the more complicated they become. It has been said by some wise humans that we should strive for simplicity. But it has never been quite clear to me what they think we should be striving for. I have stressed, I hope, that although Mr Potts had simple ways and that his lifestyle was a model of simplicity, it certainly does not follow that he was a simple man. I suppose I mean that Mr Potts was content with the simple things in life, I mean the things that most people don't even notice doing because they're in too much of a hurry – like eating and drinking. After all, who really takes the time to notice what they eat and drink? – though perhaps for much of the time what they eat and drink is hardly worth noticing at all. For most people on their way to work in the morning or taking a lunch-break, it's mostly a matter of down-the-hatch and out-the-door. That's why most people don't even taste what they eat and drink. For so many, the whole point of drinking alcohol is to get tipsy and the whole point of coffee is to help them keep going. (Actually it's become a kind of ritual – first, alcohol to become inebriated, followed by coffee to get them back on their feet!) And then there are those who either have no breakfast at all or eat it on the hoof.

(With the word 'hoof', I am not, of course, referring to horses. I myself should hate to eat anything on a horse's hoof – it couldn't possibly improve the taste, and the horse wouldn't, in any case, stay still long enough to get through the first course. No, I am simply saying that many people eat while doing other things, like rushing to catch trains.)

Mr Potts took his time and relished what he ate and drank, and he never ate or drank to excess. It is worth elaborating on a point previously mentioned, that it's just when things are done to excess that simplicity ends and complications begin. This is one lesson that Mr Potts didn't require to be taught by the Elves. For so many of us, when it comes to life's little pleasures and peccadilloes, it's a question of all or nothing at all. But Mr Potts knew very well that, within reason, the less you have of something you like or the less you do something you like doing, the more you enjoy it when you have it or do it and the more special it becomes, and that when something ceases to be special it hardly seems worth having or doing and might even descend to the status of harmful addiction, the point where pleasure surrenders to lamentable necessity. Pleasurable things become painful when overindulged, even to the extent that continued indulgence may prove fatal. Like the Elves, Mr Potts knew that a little goes a long way, and too much stops short of contentment. The Elves, like the wise of old, know all about that monster called Nemesis.

But as for simplicity of *mind*, Mr Potts had none of it. I was, on occasion, tempted to tell him that he had a tendency to think too much, especially about the more regrettable, unchanging and unchangeable features of the 'human condition'. I never did tell him in just these words. He would, I think, never have agreed. Nonsense! I *know very well* that he would have disagreed! – and very strongly at that. I know this because I once mentioned the subject in reference to someone else. He gave me an intense look with those penetrating blue eyes of his (did I mention that he had penetrating blue eyes? – well, he did!) and then ignored me for the rest of the morning and refused to respond when I offered him the last piece of toast on the plate. I left feeling guilty of some heinous crime. But he was alright again the next time round – though the subject of thinking too much was never broached again.

But his icy response did prompt me to give the subject of thinking some thought. I concluded, rather sheepishly, that it makes no sense to speak of thinking too much about important things – it would be like saying that you can love someone too much, when love is really love and not some ridiculous obsessive substitute, some imposter that fools us into thinking it's something worth feeling – I am reminded about those flowers without aroma pretending to be roses. I suppose we can think too much when we think very wrongly, but that's like saying that you can love too much when really what you're feeling is not love at all but something quite different, some form of obsession maybe.

But I gave up thinking about thinking. I think you can see why. I'm quite content to agree with Mr Potts that you can't think too much about things that matter. And that's that. It's enough to say that the simplicity I found in Mr Potts's little habits, his daily lifestyle and routine, were not matched by what must have been going on inside that head of his.

(When I say 'going on inside that head of his', I don't mean that something was happening as it might be happening if you put kittens inside a cardboard-box. The mind is not a box, cardboard or otherwise. I just mean 'what he was thinking'.)

Given that thinking, in the deeper sense, is so unpopular and so rare, it's really amazing that there are still people who are paid to think and to help others to do likewise. They are called philosophers. They are, however, few in number, as are those who wish to be taught how to think. Humans with a philosophical bent are commonly regarded as weird and eccentric beings with little or no practical good sense. This is because philosophy from time immemorial has been regarded as an impractical cerebral activity, one with no practical consequences, as though philosophers and their students spend all their time in their armchairs gazing at the ceiling and conjuring up all sorts of speculative theories which have no bearing whatsoever on the practicalities of life. It is, of course, quite clear that such critics have no idea how to think, for it fails to occur to them that thinking, in particular of the deeper kind, has been, still is, and will always be the bedrock of *action*. Many lives have been lost, and many also saved, in the name of ideologies of various kinds or flavours: Nazism, Communism, Christianity, Judaism, Islamism, Humanism, Democracy, Egalitarianism, to name just a few. And ideologies, at least in the first instance, are the fruit of thinking – of the deeper kind. I suppose what's important is to think the *right* thoughts and construct the *right* ideology – if you feel you *must* have an ideology, though

I believe there is no 'must' about it! As for the more superficial kind of thinking, that which belongs to everyday, routine activities, a little more thought would very often go a long way towards the prevention of folly and hurt. But little of this ever occurs to those who put philosophers and their students down. They continue to regard philosophy and philosophers as irrelevant.

Now I know for a fact that Mr Potts, being inevitably something of a philosopher himself, had much respect for the thinkers of old. I spotted several books on his bookshelf, some dialogues of Plato I believe – and there's nothing like these to show you what thinking is all about. Plato, in the *Republic*, criticises those who believe philosophy to be of no 'practical' value – and he does a pretty good job of it. Anyway, Plato, and of course Mr Potts himself, would both be considered irrelevant old duffers dressed in togas and tweedy jackets who have no useful role in the land of the living apart from their being objects of amusement and comic diversion. Well, I suppose it just goes to show that when hard thinking, as distinct from blind propaganda, is relegated to the nursery, the world goes to pot.

Chapter Nine

THE OUTSIDER

I suppose, if Mr Potts was in fact irrelevant, we might say that he lived in a world of his own, or that he lived *in* the world but was not *of* the world. Either way, he certainly isolated himself from the living as much as he possibly could – stopping short, as we have already said, of taking up residence in a tent somewhere in the sticks and far from the madding crowd. In another place and another time, Mr Potts might have become a mountain man, if we imagine his house of stone replaced by a wooden hovel. But as it was, his refusal to follow the crowd, to go with the flow and to toe the line, meant that his channels of communication with the rest of the world were severely limited, not of course that he voiced any complaint – on the contrary.

(It will, I hope, be readily understood that the words 'crowd', 'flow' and 'toe' are not to be taken literally. The reference is not to a crowd of football fans, for example. And flow is not really the flow of a river, and toe does not refer to Mr Potts's feet, which were, as far as I could tell, as unremarkable as the rest of him.)

He hadn't even a landline telephone, let alone a 'smart' phone, not even a television. You will remember that his television was interred in a hole at the bottom of the garden – respectfully, to mark, for old time's sake, what television had once been and had been intended to be, not of course for what it had become. He knew nothing about emails and passwords, let alone social media. If asked, he would probably have hazarded a guess that 'Facebook' was all about facial cosmetics, which, come to think of it, would not have been wholly untrue, and the only 'tik-tok' he would have acknowledged was that of the old grandfather clock which stood, precariously it must be said, in his hallway, while 'tweeting' would have been something that birds do. And so, his house had none of the clutter of modern technology. He was, in short, commonly regarded as an antiquated man, incomprehensibly and unforgivably quite out of step with the times.

I did buck up the courage to ask him how he could possibly manage in a world which depends so heavily on such a clutter of wires and gadgetry, forgetting momentarily that he was not really *of* this world at all. Anyway, he answered in generalities, as any philosopher worth his salt would have been expected to do, stating that technology is a form of entrapment and enslavement, that technology should be likened to an unbridled beast that forges ahead of its own accord neither consulting people in general nor taking into account whether everyone affected by it wishes to go along with it. Technology, he insisted, dictates that you are either with it or against it for 'in-betweeners' aren't tolerated. There is no happy medium, he explained, and if you're against it, you're considered an outsider and cast out into a kind of social oblivion.Mr Potts had obviously opted to be an outsider. He finished his tirade by saying that technology, as we know it today, simply gives a further dimension to crime, providing a smooth channel for the more unwelcome fruits of human kind. On another occasion, he remarked that he would have liked to write a book entitled *The Dictatorship of Technology* but that he was hampered by a lack of knowledge of what he called the 'inner workings' of the very dictator the book would have sought to denounce! (I thought this rather curious. After all, it's quite possible, for example, to criticise motorised traffic for its devastating effects on the environment, and for the loss of life, not to mention the life-changing injuries, it causes, without knowing much, if anything, about how a combustion engine works! In fact, the vast majority of critics are in this very camp. In any case, the validity of Mr Potts's general outpourings against technology weren't in the slightest affected by his ignorance of 'inner workings'. But, I suppose, writing something voluminous about it is something else – or, at least, he seemed to think so.)

Pondering later upon his words, it occurred to me that if Mr Potts was right about the negative effects of technology, it would be a further argument in favour of the simple life, in favour of simplicity – which is to say, a life free from the jargon, clutter and complications that technology involves, and free, not of all crime (which would be a silly and confused expectation), but of the opportunities technology provides for cyber crime to flourish, and free also from military technology, which threatens the existence both of this world and the world which, according to Mr Potts, the Elves inhabit. Of course, we can carry on as we are and hope for a change of heart, for an astonishing improvement in human nature, but this seems as absurd as the expectation that someday all crime will cease to exist. If one day all crime ceased to exist, it would be because human beings ceased to exist, as Mr Potts would undoubtedly have pointed out.

I must say, the more I thought about it, the more I sympathised with Mr Potts's position concerning technology. Of course, there are those who will insist that communication has improved significantly due to technological innovation. But they never seem to ask questions about the *quality* of what is communicated, nor do they say much about the burgeoning and virtually untouchable *criminality* of communications. People will say that we go along with a changing world, but sadly some changes are decidedly for the worse, and changes for the better are hardly ever unreservedly so. And yet, many humans persist in speaking of change as though it's necessarily a good thing, and that's very silly – it would be like saying that every holiday is a good thing, when we know very well that some holidays are total disasters and that we'd have been infinitely better off staying home.

As a consequence of Mr Potts's dismissive attitude towards the technology which most other people had long since come to consider indispensable, there was no place in his vocabulary for the jargon technology brings with it. This I have already said. But it has just occurred to me that philosophers themselves, amongst whom, as I have also said, we should most probably count Mr Potts himself, are quite fond of jargon and of words which have '- ism' at the end of them. And I wonder whether they would be happy to speak of Mr Potts's 'isolation*ism*' to describe his refusal to go with the flow and toe the line. Now it has been said that only dead fish swim with the tide, and I must explain immediately that this is not a reference to what real fish do or do not do. It is simply an expression that is meant to criticise the mentalities of people who are either incapable or unwilling to question whether what most people consider either right or wrong really *is* right or wrong in logic or in morals, in the heart or in the head. The thing is, once you start to question things, you begin to feel *outside* them and *detached* from them, and this feeling is perhaps akin to the detachment that Buddhists speak of. You begin to see the world from, as it were, the outside, if that makes any sense. However, that may be, I rather think that if we want to speak of Mr Potts's isolationism we must see it as a result of his refusal to accept *blindly* or on face value what the majority of people take very much for granted.

(Please note that the word 'blindly' is not a reference to eyesight but to a lack of questioning, and 'face value' has nothing to do with cosmetic surgery, but is another way of talking about how things seem when looked at superficially.)

So, it's like this, that Mr Potts could tell the difference between a thing being unquestioned and its being unquestionable, or a thing being uncontested and its being incontestable, which is a distinction that those who follow everyone else like sheep find it hard or impossible to grasp. The very act of questioning what so many people take for granted seems to give the questioner a feeling of isolation or detachment from the things questioned and from the people who never think of questioning them at all. Think of the simplest proposition, say 'a=a', – mathematicians never question its validity, but as soon as they ask questions about concepts like mathematical identity and equation they become philosophers as well and they begin to see such propositions from the 'outside'. Once they start questioning the concept of 'equation' they are questioning the whole of mathematics, and they begin to see mathematics from the 'outside' as well. By the way, to question something is not necessarily to criticise or reject it. I might question whether I should wear my purple shirt, but this doesn't mean that I'm about to throw it into the dustbin. When philosophers question things they are seeking to understand them better, and the results of their analyses may or may not entail suggestions about what to do with the things they have analysed.

(Note that to follow others *like* sheep, does not mean that they *are* sheep. People are not really sheep, any more than someone who looks at you sheepishly has the face of one of these delightfully woolly creatures.)

Well, I'm quite sure I'm right to understand Mr Potts's isolationism in this way. But it's not the whole story – or at least Mr Potts would say it isn't. It was on one of those rare occasions when Mr Potts's opened up to me during a tea and toast morning.

(When I say 'opened up' I don't mean that he revealed the inner workings of his body. I mean that he began to speak more openly about himself and his past.)

He said something quite strange. He said it all started, or so he thought, after the death of his dear wife. She was, he said, his whole world, and he had often wondered how he would possibly go on living without her after her demise, if, that is, she happened to pass away before he did, and it was his fervent wish that he would go first. The dreaded day came when she departed this world, leaving him alone to deal with it. And after the very few guests finished paying their respects on the day of the funeral and left him alone in the house, and his children tearfully left with their partners to, as the cliché has it, 'get on with their own lives', Mr Potts really did wonder just how he would be able to carry on.

Now it was at this point that his narrative was not at all easy to understand, and I'm not at all sure I've got it right – but I couldn't possibly have asked him to go over it all again, no I wouldn't have had the heart to do it. (Please note that here 'heart' is not a reference to anything cardiac.) Anyway, I'll do my best to recall what he told me, whether or not it makes much sense. Well, according to Mr Potts, with his beloved Mrs Potts gone and the house now empty and himself already at the very end of his wits, he suddenly began to see things differently. I say 'things', but what I really mean is people, other *people*! Suddenly they ceased to be a species of being he could recognise or recognise comfortably. Other people suddenly became 'humans', I mean as though 'human' meant being a member of another species of being – in other words, they took on the aspect of strange creatures, as though they were from another planet entirely. It was not at all a pleasant experience. He noted that they are two appendages called 'arms' and two more, longer and upright, called 'legs'. They had heads which enabled them to think, or at least think to some very limited extent. And upon their heads they wore strands, sometimes long and sometimes short, called 'hair'. They had two bulges on the front of their faces which they called 'eyes' and something protruding called 'noses' and under these noses they had cavities, 'mouths', which they filled in order to sustain themselves. They also had two more protrusions called 'ears' which enabled them to hear one another, or to hear one another when they were in a rare mood to listen. These creatures seemed to walk, rather glide at different speeds, from one place to another. Above all, they had a most unfortunate leaning towards aggression, violence and contention in their attitudes to and their dealings with one another. These creatures, called 'human beings', spent their lives coming and going, though many had no idea at all whether they were coming or going, and they were born and passed away like the leaves that grow on trees and fall in the autumn.

It was all, he said, very baffling, and very sad. But, as for Mr Potts himself, he was left as though he were on the outside looking in, as though the whole world and its human inhabitants were inside one gigantic glass enclosure and he was on the outside peering inside it. And when he looked in the long mirror in his bedroom he was amazed to see that he looked exactly the same as all those strange and unhappy creatures. He said he started to laugh and couldn't stop laughing, not, I think, because he found the comparison very pleasing but because he found it absurd. He was one of *them*, at least to all appearances. But he didn't *feel* one of them, no not at all. He wasn't at all sure whether they were from another planet, or whether he himself was. All he knew was that he was isolated from everyone else, and this isolation gave him mixed feelings of relief and loneliness. It was perhaps a measure of his loneliness and sense of isolation that he spoke to *things*, as well as to birds and hedgehogs, as though they were sentient and could understand him. As he finished sweeping the patio, I once heard him say, 'Well, thanks a million. That's a job well done,' fondly addressing his sweeping brush. On another occasion, he seemed to be in dispute with his washing machine as to whether or not it was time for it to retire!

I must say, I still fail to understand any of this. Nor can I account for the fact that he seemed to have made room for me in his life if this was the way he felt about everyone else. Mind you, and as I think I've already said but must now repeat, although I counted him as a friend, even if an odd specimen of a friend, I don't think he thought of me in anything like the same way. I felt I was tolerated, though why I should have been tolerated more than the rest of humanity I can't now guess. If this makes any sense to you, all very well and good – though I must say I find it quite foggy.

(When I say I find it foggy, I am not referring to the weather, which, in fact, is quite clear and bright at the moment. I mean, of course, that I find it confusing or difficult to understand.)

But one huge advantage of his feeling of isolation from the rest of humanity, I hazard to guess, is that it enabled him to go on living despite the momentous loss of his beloved wife, to go on living alone, and to do so while ignoring the unkind judgement of others that he must be potty. If they thought him potty, they were acknowledging that he was different from themselves – and this would have suited Mr Potts down to the ground, because it was, of course, a view which exactly coincided with his own, being a view that he thrived on and which kept him going.

And so, despising the world he saw around him, Mr Potts slipped into a world of his own. I say 'slipped' because it was not as if he made any conscious decision to either create such a world or to enter into it. Not at all. No, it was rather as if it came to him in the way that a letter addressed to you comes through the letter box, assuming that you didn't send it to yourself! You feel obliged to open it whether you want to or not. It is, as it were, thrust upon your attention and there's nothing you can do about it. But here the comparison ends. Because you can decide to ignore the letter, burn it or throw it away. But Mr Potts was powerless to do anything of the sort. The world he now saw around him was fixed and unchangeable and it gave him an equally fixed and unchangeable sense that he was different and outside it all. But the realisation that he was different, outside it all and in a world of his own was a most welcome release. It struck him how odd, how silly, how foolish, how mindless and empty-headed all those strange creatures were to live their lives in conflict with one another. What they did to one another was hard to watch, like the things on television that seemed to advertise and promote their contempt for one another. But now he could switch them all off, as though it were all on television, because it was not *his* world, and he wanted nothing of it. The world to which he had once belonged was a desert. Now he had found, or had thrust upon him, an oasis in a sea of sand. And in all this, or so he would strongly maintain, the Elves had played no small part.

From the very moment Mr Potts stepped out of the world of humans and into his own he felt sure that the Elves were watching him, not with any evil intent but, on the contrary, because they were looking out for him. By separating himself off from the ghastly world of humans, he had, as it were, taken a firm step towards that of the Elves – I say a step, because, as I've said more than once, it is quite impossible for anyone to enter fully into the world of the Elves. No, the Elves are far too circumspect and far too choosey to let any Tom, Dick or Harry walk right in and assume the identity of an Elf at the drop of a hat.

(Let it be duly and respectfully noted that when I use the names 'Tom', 'Dick' and 'Harry' I am not now referring to specific individuals with these names, as though I were saying, 'I'm not sure who's responsible, but it's either Tom, Dick, or Harry'. I am just saying that the Elves would never allow *just anyone* to fancy himself as an Elf. In the same way, when I say 'at the drop of a hat' I'm not really talking about hats, as if I were to add that hats are out of the question but gloves may be acceptable, so that if a pair of gloves were to be dropped instead of a hat it would be alright. No, the expression 'at the drop of a hat' means 'just like that!' I hope I've not made myself too obscure, though I've always thought that a little obscurity is a fine thing, since it focuses the mind concerning the complexities of language.)

As I was saying, when Mr Potts stepped inside a world of his own he was, quite unexpectedly, opening the door, just a very little, on that of the Elves. Now, although Mr Potts hadn't expected such a thing to happen, for he had taught himself to entertain no expectations about Elves or anything else, he was somehow convinced that *they* were expecting *him*. It's as though they had prepared a room for him, or perhaps it would be better to say an ante-room – and it may be that they were so intrigued by Mr Potts that they had decided to test him out and observe him more closely. Or it's as though Mr Potts had embarked on a remarkable journey and had gone so far as to climb into a train compartment with a small suitcase – not really, of course, but it was a kind of journey all the same, one that was to take place somewhere inside his head.

I say the Elves had been and still were *observing* him. It's strikes me that there's a great deal of observing in the world of humans, and much of it, if not most of it, is done for highly questionable motives. Mr Potts, for example, was under constant surveillance by his neighbours, for they were constantly on the lookout for the latest instance of eccentricity so that they could have something to laugh about when they met in the pub. In fact, the more beer they imbibed, the more eccentric Mr Potts would seem and the more they laughed, and the more they laughed, the more they imbibed. Although Mr Potts was quite unaware of the fact, his existence was highly profitable to the landlord of *The Forlorn Pig*. Apart from such pecuniary matters, Mr Potts also provided a subject that not only tended to bring people together but to make them feel a lot cleverer and infinitely more sane than Mr Potts himself. In short, he made them feel much better about themselves. His critics, defamers and detractors lost little sleep, not to say little sheep, over the thought that the enormous benefits they enjoyed were due to his very existence. His beneficiaries were not pained by their consciences, for the simple reason that their consciences hardly ever saw the light of day on any subject under the sun or moon. They were hardly to be blamed, for it's a very pleasant thing indeed to live in the world of humans, untroubled by conscience on all matters great and small and, instead, to invite others to examine their *own* consciences – it makes for a great economy of pain and personal inconvenience.

However, to return to the main point, Mr Potts was closely observed by the Elves, because they were intrigued by his, for want of a better word, other-worldliness. And, for far less amiable motives, he was observed by his neighbours. As for Mr Potts himself, he could hardly have failed, poor fellow, to observe the goings-on in the world of humans, and the only way he could observe the Elves is through the portal of untroubled sleep. The observation that he had entered into a world of his own no doubt encouraged the Elves to seek him out in his sleep. Well, from their perspective, it was the next obvious step, and the *only* next step if they were sufficiently intrigued to want to communicate with him. After all, they could hardly be expected to jump down out of their leafy abodes and conduct an interview with him in his very own garden. To have revealed themselves in this way would have been the end of it, for we know very well that humans find it hard to comprehend differences. Had the neighbours caught sight of thin, green-clad beings hopping about Mr Potts's garden, they would no doubt have alerted the police, the army and the secret service without a first thought, let alone a second one. And Mr Potts may himself have been so shocked at the sight that he might have tumbled back into the world of humans again and been carted off to a lunatic asylum, never more to see the light of day. It's a point worth making that Elves are never to be seen in lunatic asylums, for they are deadly against the use of narcotics and amphetamines or any other human and unnatural concoctions designed to restore sanity. It' not what humans *call* sanity that interests the Elves – quite the contrary. It's what humans call *insanity* that interests them. And that's because they think humans have got things the wrong way round, having observed other things that humans have got upside down and back to front – I mean times when humans speak of love and mean by it anything but what the Elves would call love, or when they speak of peace and mean what the Elves would call war, or when they speak of freedom and mean by it anything but what the Elves would call liberty. I think I may have made myself obscure again, but it's not at all easy to understand the Elves without encountering some fog, as Mr Potts repeatedly warned me.

Now it needs to be said that the crude expression 'lunatic asylum' is not at all acceptable to the more sensitive souls amongst humans and was replaced by 'mental hospital' or 'mental institution' in an attempt to acknowledge the fact that mental derangements and indispositions of all sorts are species of *illness* and that those who suffer from them should not also suffer any social stigmas. Quite right, too! Indeed, in some cases, even the word 'mental' is left out and only the word 'hospital' remains – well, the whole thing is well-intentioned, no doubt.

But whatever such places are called, the Elves were especially worried that Mr Potts wasn't carted off to one of them, allegedly for his own safety or the safety of others. For this reason they were acutely aware of the difference between eccentricity and complete lunacy. A few eccentricities are one thing, but if Mr Potts had gone around brandishing a sword and calling himself Napoleon, intent upon finding someone, *anyone*, whom he thought was Wellington, and demanding retribution for his defeat at Waterloo – well, that would have been another matter entirely, and the Elves themselves might have agreed, most reluctantly, of course, that he should be locked away for the good of all, and especially for the good of someone who might strike Mr Potts as the very incarnation of the Duke himself, alias Mr Arthur Wellesley, for the Elves, and particularly the Elders, were nothing if not reasonable.

It is for this very reason of safeguarding Mr Potts from the possibility of being carted off to complete obscurity that the Elves decided to make their appearance on the stage of Mr Potts's world – at least in his dreams. The medicine Mr Potts needed, which could never be found within the walls of an institution, was a mixture of courage and strength, for these are the basis of hope. Now hope, as we have already somewhere mentioned, is a rare enough commodity amongst the Elves themselves, I mean when it comes to hopes concerning the betterment of human nature. But they were aware that beautiful flowers can make their appearance even in a garden neglected and overrun with weeds. They were aware of the *beauty* humans can achieve – it's just that humans don't achieve nearly enough of it. What is needed when you consider the horrible things that humans do to one another is courage and strength – they must come together, because the one without the other is useless. Anyway, when you have them together, you have a recipe for hope. Without them, hope is very difficult, and I should say impossible. Without them, 'hope' just becomes a word, and it's no good just repeating the word over and over, because if you do that it will lose all meaning, and then you just become a kind of human parrot – saying things over and over, and so not really *saying* them at all, but just producing a sound. (Can you really *say* anything if the words you use have no *meaning*?)

Anyway, this whole subject came up one morning over tea and toast. You know by now what Mr Potts was like. He would come out with a single sentence or make a single statement, and it all depended on his mood whether he would explain himself or let the whole thing hang in the air like a feather that floats but doesn't know where to land or knows where to land but is reluctant to do so. 'I just can't stand it!' he said, clutching a butter knife in one hand and a burnt piece of toast in the other. 'Can't stand what? Burned toast?' I ventured. 'Burned toast? Burned toast? What are you talking about!? No, no. I hate being on the very edge of a pier, especially at night, and looking down to the dark, deep water below lapping against the supports.'

With this, and with a hop, a skip and a jump, he was mumbling about the need for courage and strength and how the Elves were helping him with both. Well, after that I was able to put a patchwork of explanation together. I really do believe that his association with Elves had given him a new lift and helped to keep him going after his divorce from the world of humans. After all, it's not easy to keep going when you are daily and acutely aware of the bad things humans do and so thinly informed about the good. The Elves had stores aplenty of courage and strength and were in a good position to supply Mr Potts with both. The Wood Elves, in particular, were in constant fear of losing their habitat. The Elves inhabited the forests when man first walked upon the earth. The forests were thick and plenty then, and the Elves had little to fear from those primitive creatures walking upright on two legs who preferred to live in caves. They lived side by side, man knowing as little of their presence as he does now. But when man gained knowledge and skill, the trouble began, with senseless wars and the destruction of vast swathes of forest by fire and heavy artillery. There was indeed a time when the Elves wished that man would do a complete job and eradicate himself from the face of the planet for good. Instead, he lingered on, fighting his wars, and when he was not killing his fellow creatures he was cutting down the forests, those large areas wiser men called the lungs of the earth. Bad habits die hard, which is why now the earth itself is threatened with destruction from constant abuse, a by-product of what man calls civilisation – his factories, which darken the skies with their toxic fumes, his ignorance and his insatiable greed for wealth and what he calls 'economic growth'. Yes, the Elves must be forgiven if their optimism was and continues to be of the most cautious kind, for they have learned through bitter experience and tragic loss that man is not to be trusted with his words alone.

This limping caution is shared by the trees themselves, for the trees feel fear, which they communicate to the Elves, for only the Elves can read the shivering leaves and the creaking branches that tremble with unrest and foreboding. Only the Elves can share the pain of the forests. It is for the trees and for themselves that the Elves fear most those humans with their noisy chain-saws, which burst upon the air like the rat-a-tat machine guns of human warfare, and they are forever on their guard, for, in a world where forests are continually under threat, only courage and strength can comfort them in their every-weakening hope for a quiet and unmolested life for themselves and future generations – for it is for unborn Elves that they fear the most, as the better sort of humans fear for their children and their children's children and for the many generations to come – if they are to come at all. The Elders amongst the Elves tell them all to hope, but amongst themselves their faces are as grim as their thoughts. True, to the Elves is given eternal life, but who in their right senses would wish upon himself eternal misery?

It was essential that Mr Potts was never institutionalised, because he represented, for the Elves at least, the better kind of human. They planted their hopes in the Mr Pottses of the world of men, and so it was quite logical that they should wish to preserve him intact by saving him from the total oblivion which institutionalisation would have entailed. He was already widely considered an eccentric, but the Elves were intent upon damage limitation, and it really does seem that there was no one he could have looked to other than the Elves for any sympathy and consideration due to him.

This business of saving Mr Potts from institutionalisation is, you must understand, conjecture on my part, because my friend had said no such thing, and he might even have considered me quite mad in suggesting it. But in my efforts to make sense of my friend and his relationship with the Elves, a relationship you must remember which was enjoyed by him and not by me, I feel fairly confident in hazarding a guess. In fact, I can take my theorising a little further. I have asked myself why Mr Potts in particular? I mean, even if he was, as I am quite sure he was, one of the better examples of human being, how on earth could he, a single individual, have made a difference? – especially when we bear in mind the hostile nature of the world of humans. My own answer, which I force upon no one, is that the important advances made by humans have been the result of individuals forcing their attentions upon the masses that surround them, individuals in science and the arts, in medicine, in music, in politics and in social life – Newton and Einstein in physics, Wittgenstein in philosophy, Bach, Beethoven and Mozart in music, Mandela and Ghandi in social justice and civil rights, the abolitionists Wilberforce, Clarkson, Lincoln, some of the most notable abolitionists of the institution of slavery ... and the list goes on. And there are those who have given the masses blueprints on how to live and examples of what courage means: Socrates, Christ and many others, of course, who have not been captured in the limelight of history and therefore have been either quite unknown or relatively unknown to the rest of us. Individuals like these have made their impressions on others and have taken a significant number with them. The rule seems to be, individuals first and then, with luck, others follow. Such individuals display a trinity of courage, strength and humanity – all three are virtuous requirements to enable a significant advance in human civilisation to take place, but those that would follow such individuals must absorb their virtues in some form of osmosis if real and lasting progress is to be made and the tragedy of failed revolutions are to be avoided.

And Mr Potts? Was he such an individual? Did he possess to a sufficient degree this trinity of courage, strength and humanity to make a positive difference? Well, it's only a theory, and how should I know whether or not it's a valid one? After all, I wasn't privy to the minds of the Elves. But since I couldn't ask them (or ask Mr Potts for that matter, for fear of being considered madder than he was and of being chased out of the house with a kitchen mop in consequence), my only recourse is to ask myself and see what my addled brain can come up with. But if he *was* the kind of individual who could have changed things for the better, perhaps the Elves were waiting for evidence and believed that it was well worth the wait. Of course, I can't possibly say one way or the other. I wait, with the Elves, in limbo and with no more than a modicum of anticipation for confirmation of the view that the world would change significantly for the better if it were populated by very many more people like Mr Potts. Naturally, I share the view that Mr Potts was in any case far better off *outside* a mental hospital than he would have been inside one! Inside one, he would have been forever lost to humanity, whether or not he was the extraordinary individual I have always imagined him to be.

I must say, I do feel very uncomfortable not having been able to raise these matters directly and fully with Mr Potts himself. He was very much a creature of mood and did not enter into anything remotely resembling a proper explanation of things unless he felt like it, and he very rarely felt like it, and I suppose that came from living in a world of his own. It also strikes me that if Mr Potts was the kind of chap to get things done for the better, it would have entailed his having to step back into the world of humans big time! If this meant saying farewell to the Elves of his dreams, it seems a very 'iffy' proposition. I suppose the Elves would have had to send him packing, making it known to him that he had both the ability and the duty to get things done. If he ever could have got things done, it would clearly have benefited the Elves themselves. As things stood, though, the only connection Mr Potts had with the world of humans that he could relish was the tea and toast he consumed regularly for breakfast. It seems quite unrealistic to have imagined him engaging in the affairs of humans without being made a laughing stock – that's the problem when you're widely considered to be quite potty. Can anyone really be thought quite potty and at the same time make important changes for the better in the world of his detractors?

(We should perhaps clarify, in passing, a point of language. If we speak of a 'lunatic asylum' or a 'mental hospital', we don't mean that the asylum is mad or that the hospital is mental, because that would be like supposing that the asylum and the hospital are themselves humans. These phrases just describe the *kind* of hospital it is, namely one that treats humans with mental disorders. The point may seem trivial, but it is one worth making, for, as I have subsequently discovered, the Elves were for some time of the opinion that the hospital *itself* is *non compos mentis*, a belief that may still be in vogue among both the wiser Elders and some extraordinarily enlightened humans.)

Chapter Ten

BREAKFAST IN THE SNOW

If I'm right, and I'm not at all sure that I am, that the Elves believed Mr Potts to be something special and that they were entertaining the hope that he might make a positive difference in and to the world of humans, I am bound to ask myself what it is exactly they would have expected him to *do*! I am sure that if there was really something that could be done, he would have been up to the mark. Mr Potts was very simple, but he was no simpleton. Yes, but this is not what worries me.

What worries me is what Mr Potts might have been expected to do which had not been done or at least seriously attempted already, and what he might have been expected to say that had not been said already. In one important sense, he had already done more than very many humans, and here we might speak of his '*negative* value'. By this I mean that he did *not*, for example, pollute the atmosphere by means of his lifestyle: he disliked flying and *never* flew, he was careful about the food he ate, being almost vegetarian, he *didn't* even drive a car, he *didn't* lay waste vast tracks of forest, he *didn't* own factories that pollute the atmosphere, the rivers and the sea. What's more, he was *not at all* a violent man, he had *no* criminal record (as far as I know), he bought only what he needed, in particular tea and toast, he made no wars, he caused *no* disturbance. His criticism of humans was general and universal, depending *not at all* on creed, religion, culture or colour. A black man once said that the devil is white. Mr Potts would said that the devil is white, black, yellow and red – in fact, any colour that accords with his evil intentions, just as that two-horned fellow is said to cite Scripture for his purpose. The devil is a chameleon, assuming any colour that he deems appropriate for the given moment. The shortcomings of humans are, he might have said, 'built in' or, to use terms which have by now assumed an alarming currency, they are 'systemic', 'structural' or 'integral' to the human machine. Quite simply, humans are endowed with a nature that leaves a very great deal to be desired, and that's what he would have said, though perhaps not in so many words. I say 'simply', but nothing is as complex as a thing that is called simple. Perhaps the word 'simple' and its derivatives should carry a hazard warning. I must confess I am still pulled to and fro on this question of simplicity. On the one hand, I feel that we should simplify simplicity, by asking what we *mean* by it. On the other hand, I also feel that anyone who needs to ask what simplicity is has already lost the plot! However, since I lack Mr Potts's analytical powers, I must leave matters where they stand and continue as if the whole matter were crystal clear and therefore in no need of debate.

To continue, Mr Potts's needs were simple and few. If everyone were like Mr Potts, there would be no climate crisis, no wanton or excessive cutting down of trees, no wars, and nothing much at all for the Elves to worry about – they might die of boredom, but not from a lack of suitable habitat due to human failings. No, the Elves, and for that matter the rest of us, might learn to be content and live contentedly ever after. (I'm not quite sure about *happily* ever after – well, because happiness is so often assumed to require a measure of excess, and there was nothing excessive about Mr Potts, except the *absurd* simplicity (here's that word again!) and the *abject* boredom that others might attribute to him. A lady once remarked, when commenting on the life of Mr Potts, that she'd rather be dead than bored, little realising that she was dead already, for boredom is impossible for anyone with even just a modicum of curiosity, though even curiosity might become excessive – yes, but *boring*?! Even so, a common judgement against Mr Potts might well have been that he had wasted his life, that he had forgotten, if he had ever known at all, how it should be lived, or, indeed, that he believed that life itself was vastly over-valued, for what we may consider to be his 'negative value' would be in *their* eyes no value at all! In short, they might have said that his life was as unremarkable as his appearance: short, lumpy and nondescript. This is what *they* might well have said of him. The Elves, of course, might well have had a contrary opinion. I say 'of course', but I can only hazard a guess on the basis of what Mr Potts said about them and the relationship he seemed to enjoy with them. I shall be accused of sheer guesswork. I know guessing is an uncertain and hazardous business, but it has to be undertaken in the circumstances in which I find myself – attempting to say something meaningful and valid about someone who seemed to have far less interest in me than I had in him.

Well, it seems that Mr Potts's uncommon 'simplicity', as I call it, prevented him from becoming anyone of public note, like a politician, let alone a statesman of international standing. That was a problem, because it's only politicians of standing that are ever listened to – of course, I would consider seriously the judgement that politicians are seldom listened to, and listened to least of all by fellow politicians. I might go further and say that it's only fanatical politicians that ever seem to get anything done, and then, almost invariably, what they get done would have been far better left *un*done! Whatever he was, Mr Potts was not a fanatic. No, it's precisely human forms of fanaticism that turned him off the world of humans altogether and launched him into a world of his own. There are, of course, politicians who start off on the right foot, but the more successful they become in attracting the attention of the masses, the more fanatical they get, the more self-assured, and there are few things more dangerous than an excess of self-assurance.

(You will, of course, realise that when I say 'start off on the right foot' no reference is intended to real feet, as if to say it would be better to start off on the left foot because you have a bunion on your right foot and walking is painful. 'Starting off on the right foot' only means 'making a good start'.)

Here we once again bump up against an old acquaintance which is never far from the scene of the crime – human nature. People who start out with a voice loud enough to be heard curiously acquire one which is even louder, indeed deafening and offensive to more moderate ears. Now who was it who said that power tends to corrupt and absolute power corrupts absolutely? It was none other than that old friend of Mr Potts, Lord Acton. (I say 'friend', but what I mean is that Mr Potts and that historian might well have agreed on this matter had they lived at the same time and somehow got to know one another – they are in any case friends in spirit, especially since they shared a special interest in the history of ancient Rome.) The trouble begins when power is mixed with human nature, a toxic compound, to which very few, if any, are immune. It's been said that Saint Augustine shed tears at his appointment as Bishop of Hippo, not tears of joy or fulfilment, which might have been expected from one exalted to an important post, but tears of anguish, for he was afraid that he might become corrupted by the power that his position as bishop implied. He needn't have worried, for his simplicity of soul (what on earth do I mean by that?) saved him from corruption – and how could a man who had shed tears over the possibility of losing his soul to the world of corrupt men have ever been in danger of losing it?But Augustine was a saint, or, at the time of his appointment, a saint in the making – which at least suggests that he was a very rare breed!

Yes, for the rest of us poor mortals immunity from corruption is a rarity indeed and it's not at all certain what could bring that immunity about. *Simplicity* might do it, but then simplicity is invariably abandoned as soon as you enter the very public world of politics. (Again, that word insists upon intruding, like an evangelist who will be heard come what may!)

No, the problem is that if Mr Potts were to be actually *heard* (advocating *simplicity* let's say?!) he would have needed a loud voice, and the chances are that his voice would have become quite deafening. Mr Potts himself might well have begun to enjoy the effect it had on all and sundry, and before long his life might have become a montage of complexities, and the very simplicity he advocated would have become swallowed up inside it. Simplicity is rather like a work of art, I think. Touch it up and it's no longer a work of art – like drawing a moustache on the Mona Lisa and calling it an improvement. Talk too much about it and it becomes just another cliché – or far worse it might become a clarion call for some of the worst excesses of which humans are capable. Many of the so-called Puritans of 17th-century England had much to answer for – amongst their vices was an excess of intolerance and a fearful lack of humanity.

The Elves aren't simpletons, either. So, the question must be: did they really expect Mr Potts to bring about a fundamental and lasting change for the better in human nature, or were they more than satisfied with the kind of person he was and wished merely to preserve him in that state, wishing that all the rest of us could be the same? In other words, did they admire and respect him for his *negative value*, believing that if we were all like him the world would be a much better place? There's much to be said for this view, though sadly it did nothing to change the world for the better because Mr Potts was quite unique, and so hecontinued to live in a very imperfect world which was, and of course still is by their standards, so imperfect that they were moved to create a world of their own, a world which is nowadays as far removed from the world of men as they can possibly manage to make it.

The mind boggles, and while the mind boggles, the world continues its downward path – at least as far as climate change is concerned and given that the pundits are to be believed. But let's face it, those who talk about halting climate change, or at least reducing it to manageable levels, are assuming a very great deal – they are above all assuming that the deficiencies of human nature as we know it can be transcended to an extent much greater than any of the greatest and most respectable religions have succeeded in achieving. (I hesitate to talk about religions at all, since they seem to cause as much harm as good, and some have been and still are inimical to good will among humans, due again to our old acquaintance 'human nature'. Even the best of men, it seems, are not to be trusted utterly without reservation, and even saints would agree that they can't trust themselves. This is why, I believe, Mr Potts never raised the subject. He became very agitated around the subject of holy men, largely because he believed there weren't any. Whenever a thorny subject like this arose, he greeted it with the same old mantra: 'Leave it be – you won't draw me on this!')

(Not to cause unnecessary confusion on an already confused and confusing matter, let's make it clear at once that when Mr Potts said, 'You won't draw me on this,' he wasn't refusing to sit for his portrait or rough pencil sketch. He simply meant that he didn't want to discuss the matter.)

The Elves, of all creatures, must know how difficult it is to bring about positive, meaningful and lasting change amongst humans. I'm almost inclined to think that they were overestimating Mr Potts's abilities and underestimating the difficulties. Of course, they were aware of his willingness to attempt the extraordinary and the extraordinarily difficult. I, myself, am witness to this. It was a very cold morning in midwinter and the snow had fallen heavily the night before when Mr Potts insisted that we take morning tea and toast in the garden. He noted my shocked expression but proceeded as though he hadn't. I knew it was fruitless to attempt to talk him out of it once his mind was made up, and it was certainly made up. Out we trotted, and I was grateful that it wasn't at that same moment snowing. There we were, sitting at the small garden table in a frost-biting chill, sipping tea and toast he had carried out from the kitchen. I've heard of iced tea, but this was absurd. 'Ah! – the fresh air! Nothing like it!' he said, a remark that earned an icy nod from me. We sat there for a full half-hour while he repeated the remark as if to justify our being there. To my mind, nothing, at least nothing sane, could possibly justify it. No doubt the experience was thrilling for Mr Potts. All I can do is testify to the fact that it is no easy matter to drink tea and eat toast while at the same time wearing gloves and smothered in long, woolly scarves – Mr Potts, of course, wore a thin, short-sleeved and extremely flowery summer shirt designed for heat waves.

No doubt the Elves were well aware of the event, one which could only have supported the opinion that Mr Potts was, if not entirely and irredeemably insane, a very remarkable individual, ready to test trying circumstances without at the same time losing heart or failing to make the very best of them. They could not, of course, have said the same about me, though perhaps they were more than ready to doubt my own sanity in befriending him.

Yes, but it's one thing to take tea and toast with a touch of frostbite, and quite another to sway the hearts and minds of the vast swathes of mankind, and of course nothing short of this would save the planet from climatic disaster, not to mention wars, racial hatreds, lack of religious toleration, and such matters that either make our short lives shorter than they need be or certainly vastly more difficult than they are already. Lesser attempts would have been as fruitless as attempting to change Mr Potts himself. (Needless to say, the term 'fruitless' does not mean that we would have been deprived of apples, oranges and bananas and other even more exotic fruits should we have attempted to change Mr Potts. It just means that we would not have achieved the desired result.)

Expecting Mr Potts alone to make the world of humans a better place was of course ridiculous. No one person can do that. Even leaders need followers, and the biggest of problems need very great leaders and very many followers. Clearly, there never was a time when a leader was great enough and the numbers of his followers vast enough to put an end to the world's greatest problems, problems such as war, hunger, the abuse of the planet and the intolerance and greed that so often causes them, otherwise there would be little need to talk about them now. Conversely, there have been all too many far less beneficent leaders with their all too many followers who have had disastrous results on our planet and its inhabitants. Evil is easier to achieve than good.

Mr Potts had obviously given up hoping that such beneficent leaders and such armies of followers would one day appear out of nowhere, for nowhere is where they would have to come.

I suspect, though here again I am only guessing, that living as he did, completely without hope, let alone expectation, was an extremely painful thing and that he would rather have lived with hope, however slim it might have been. Hope is like a coat in cold weather – even a threadbare coat is better than no coat at all. Hope would have enabled him to step back into the world into which he was born, the world of humans, for it was only the world of his own making, together with his eccentricities, that kept him upright at all. I can't help feeling that the world he had created for himself was only temporary, a kind of respite and that one day he would have made a u-turn and returned to the world of humans, abandoning his twilight world of Elves and their intrusion into his dreams. But to do that he needed a leg up, some guiding star, something that would support him and never desert him – because it was just that lack of support that made him abandon the world of humans and create another, one in which he and his eccentricities might hide. But where that support would have come from, if it could ever have come at all, is impossible to say.

Chapter Eleven

THE SUPERMARKET INCIDENT

My thinking about Mr Potts is in dire need of some clarification. I think I've said somewhere that if everyone were like Mr Potts the world would be a much better place. But I think this is stretching things a bit and assuming a great deal. (Of course, when I say 'stretching', I don't mean that we should do some aerobics, just that I may be over-generalising and consequently over-simplifying things.)

Anyway, if everyone were like Mr Potts, there'd be no war, it's true, and that's a very fine thing. But also, there'd be no television, no computers, no supermarkets, no football and probably no sport of any kind, no pubs, no air travel, no cars, no cinema, no cosmetics industry, and no ... well, the list goes on and on, as you can easily imagine. The absence of these things wouldn't have worried Mr Potts one tiny bit, and it wouldn't worry anybody else if they were all like Mr Potts. They really would have to be very much like him. There would have to be a complete, or near-complete, marriage of minds between Mr Potts and the rest of humanity. Otherwise, it would be devastating for most other people, because they take these things very seriously and have grown up with them – not to mention the unemployment that the absence of these things would cause. Most people would consider Mr Potts's ideal world to be an extremely retrograde step, and stark boredom would become a widespread killer disease. If everyone were just like Mr Potts, they might well be expected to co-exist peaceably. But it's asking a bit much to expect everyone to be just like him. As things stand, the vast majority of mankind would consider Mr Potts's world to be as colourless as he was himself, as I've already said. It's very hard to imagine a world full of Mr Pottses – as though the rest of humanity were cloned, with Mr Potts as their template. If variety is the spice of life, life would be tasteless. What, they would ask, would the world be without football? And given that Mr Potts's sexual appetite appears to have been zero, if not below, they might ask the same sort of question about what they call 'love' – perhaps not about romance, since this seems to have slipped off the world's radar long ago.

No, the plain fact of the matter is that if we wanted everyone to live like Mr Potts it could only work in an entirely different world, a world we don't now know and one which, if we were able to compare it with the world we do know, we might not like at all. If we imagine that the world we know changed in an instant to accommodate Mr Potts without reservation, people would need to undergo a complete loss of memory in order to stand any chance of putting up with the dramatic and radical transitions involved, otherwise there would be revolution upon revolution and Mr Potts would be sought out, hanged, drawn and quartered, cut up into a thousand pieces and end up in tins of dog food.

The long and the short of it is that not everyone can be like Mr Potts and that it's probably a very good thing that they can't.

(When I say 'the long and the short of it' I don't mean to say that we should apply a measuring tape to the subject, which would be absurd, or for that matter that some things are short and some things are long, which of course is perfectly true but not at all enlightening. The expression is simply a synonym for 'the essential point'.)

Besides, not everything outlawed in Mr Potts's world is bad, or entirely bad. In fact, Mr Potts might well be in danger of throwing the baby out with the bathwater. For example, from the fact that football hooliganism is a bad thing it doesn't follow that football should be *abolished* – if that's the right word. Or again, from the fact that sexual abuse is obnoxious, it doesn't follow that sex is a mistake – after all, if it were given up, it might mean the phasing out of the human population altogether. I'm not quite so confident about this last possibility – I was told, on Mr Potts's authority of course, that there are those amongst the Elves who would not shed many tears if humans were to disappear from the face of the earth altogether.

Fortunately, though, it's not a view widely held amongst them, being one that is discouraged by the Elders, again according to Mr Potts.

(As a note of caution for the less astute of my readers, when I say that Mr Potts is in danger of throwing the baby out with the bathwater, I am not really talking about a baby or about bathwater. It will be agreed, I fervently hope, that no baby should be thrown out with the bathwater, or thrown anywhere at all for that matter. It is precisely this kind of mindless barbarism that has turned Mr Potts away from the entire human race and made him ashamed to be associated with it, let alone to be counted among its members. No, the expression 'to throw the baby out with the bathwater' simply means that when we reject something that should be rejected, like bathwater, we may be in danger of rejecting with it something important that should never be rejected, like a baby!)

So, it seems we'd be better off saying that the world would be a better place, not if *everyone* were like Mr Potts, but if there were *more* people like him. In other words, people need to be balanced out. I'm sure Mr Potts, with his in-depth knowledge of the ancients, would agree that when balance is sacrificed to extremes Nemesis can be expected. And it may well be that the balance should be redressed in favour of Mr Potts, for the voices raised against him are far too numerous, and I've been unable to find anyone to speak in his favour. Which is why, with a hostile public, he would somehow need to be protected against critical extravagance and the fearful steps that might be taken against him should his eccentricities be considered too far-fetched. Which brings me to an event very much involving Mr Potts which took place in the local supermarket.

It was during one of my routine morning visits. I found his front door ajar and went inside, but Mr Potts was nowhere to be seen. I looked everywhere, including the garden, and then, returning to the kitchen, found a curious note on the table, presumably intended for me. It read: 'Gone to replenish tea and toast. Back soon, if at all – depending on reception.' The first part of the note was clear. The second part made the mind boggle. Frankly, I was concerned, and, after waiting the best part of an hour, was too concerned to wait any longer. I made for the local shops, dreading what I might find.

I had every right to be concerned. It turned out that Mr Potts had bought tea and bread from a small corner shop, and then, instead of heading straight home, made the fateful decision to cross the high street to the supermarket. Once inside, it seems that he divested himself of his clothing and, standing naked on a plastic podium, on which had rested a pyramid of chocolate coated breakfast cereal, Mr Potts began to deliver a speech to the shoppers and checkout staff. It was not just that he had, with a majestic wave of his hand, upset the pyramid of cereals, but that he had upset everyone by wearing nothing but his birthday suit. People were so shocked by his lack of apparel that no-one could later give a coherent account of what he actually said, or shouted, to the crowd of shoppers. I came in at the tail end of this episode, just as a police car screeched to a halt outside. Knowing Mr Potts, I daresay he was railing against the use of chemicals and preservatives in food, or against junk food, or against the way in which the planet is being abused by unscrupulous food manufacturers. Whatever it was, it was against something that was outlawed in his own world but all too apparent in the world he was obliged to share with human beings.

(It should be reasonably clear from the above that the expression 'birthday suit' does not mean a suit of clothes that Mr Potts wore on his birthday. It means he wasn't wearing any clothes at all. That is, he was stark naked, as the day he was born.)

I arrived in the nick of time. I rushed up and covered him in my overcoat, which was thankfully long enough to hide his essentials. Then, with the police on the scene, I began the tortuous explanation of his behaviour which, I said, was due to an accumulation of stress and would be short-lived once I got him home, after which he would no doubt be more than forthcoming with his apologies. After all, no real harm had been done. It was not as though he had stolen anything or had even had any intention to do so.

(As you must know, when I say 'snapped' I don't mean that he was broken in two. I mean he had reached the limits of his mental endurance.)

It was a near thing. He wasn't taken into custody. Had they taken him he might have ended up in the funny farm. Luckily, the police and the supermarket manager were satisfied, albeit reluctantly, with my account of things, and he was allowed to go home under my supervision, though more formal apologies were expected in due course.

As you might have gathered by now, I admire Mr Potts as a man who was suffering from an excess of sanity. It was painfully ironic, therefore, that I should be appealing to a temporary bout of insanity to save him from those who are suffering from a dearth of sanity – which struck me as rather like arguing that the patient is fitter than the doctor who believes that the patient is ill. I was in the ridiculous position of having to explain that Mr Potts was in general really quite as 'normal' as the next man, when of course he was not at all like the next man. I felt I was telling a very big lie – but at least in the very best of causes. No matter, Mr Potts was at least saved from the funny farm and could return to the comparative safety of his little retreat.

(It should be noted here that 'funny farm' is an expression that means 'mental hospital' and not a farm that happens to be run by an amusing farmer or a farm where the animals tell jokes – mind you, if the animals did tell jokes, they couldn't possibly be worse or more tasteless than those humans all too often tell each other. Mr Potts, being a stickler for tastefulness, would reprimand me for using the expression. But I'm afraid it just slipped out and I couldn't get it back in again.)

So, I took Mr Potts home. On the way, he said nothing. Nor did he utter a word after I sat him down on the bed in the bedroom. He stared into space for a few minutes, then he stood up and rummaged around for his clothes, which he began to put on slowly and methodically. 'Well, if you're alright now ...' I began, making to leave. 'Perfectly,' he said, ' – *as always*!' he added, rather sarcastically, I thought. I nodded and made to go downstairs. 'Thanks, anyway,' he said. And that was that.

How awful to be suffering from a surfeit of sanity! His disapproval of humanity was so deep-seated and immoveable that hope didn't stand a chance. I mean, I had often thought of taking the bull by the horns by pointing out to him that his total condemnation of human nature was unfair, too stark and too simplistic, and that progress had been made and would no doubt continue to be made in the human condition. But the plain truth was that there was nothing I could tell him that he did not know already and knew far better than I. He had an answer for everything. I suppose if I had told him that the institution of slavery, once upon a time almost totally unquestioned, had been abolished, he would have pointed out how fragile any step forward was and that, as far as human nature was concerned, the all too widespread and incurable disease of human trafficking showed demonstrably that the seeds of retrogression were indestructible and that we need only turn our backs on the matter for a few moments for the institution to return with bells on. Faith, like trust, is so hard to restore once gone, and in Mr Potts it was very hard to find any vestiges of it. So I was at a loss what to say or do. He must surely have suffered very deeply. That said, the morning after the supermarket incident he was at the breakfast table, ready with tea and toast, and I felt it was quite out of place to make any reference to the supermarket incident. Things were normal again, or as normal as they could possibly be with Mr Potts.

(It is no doubt needless to point out that when I spoke above of 'taking the bull by the horns' I was not suggesting for a moment that I should have done a spot of bull-fighting, a sport which quite frankly I find abhorrent. Nor do I wish to give the impression that I am physically equipped for such a task, even if the occasion presented itself through some kind of unwelcome necessity. No, it is of course simply an expression that means 'tackling an awkward problem' or 'confronting a difficult matter'.)

I rather think that Mr Potts had been deeply impressed with the doings of Socrates, who had questioned matters in the marketplace. Mr Potts had, in the absence of a marketplace, decided to pursue things in the local supermarket instead. Had Mr Potts lived at the time of Socrates he might have suffered a similar fate to that august philosopher and might have paid the ultimate price for rocking the boat. Were Socrates living in our time and were he to cause a commotion in a supermarket, he might be obliged to spend a little time in the company of an analyst or, at worst, be detained at His Majesty's Pleasure, awaiting a psychiatric report – this might be regarded by many as indisputable proof that humans have made significant moral progress since ancient Athens, though whether it speaks for an advanced morality in the generality or for sheer expediency in the particular case is not immediately clear.

(It's no doubt worth pointing out that 'rocking the boat' does not literally mean the act of purposely destabilising a vessel on turbulent waters. It's simply a figure of speech meaning to question or criticise something in a way that makes others feel uncomfortable or in some way threatened. Similarly, someone who is detained at His Majesty's Pleasure is not delayed at the palace either forcibly or by circumstances prevailing – it's just a figure of speech meaning that the person in question is in jail and is there whether or not His Majesty is aware of the fact, which he probably isn't.)

Chapter Twelve

HOPES DASHED

Well, there was one occasion when you could have blown me down! (I don't mean by this that you could have stood me at the end of a garden leaf-blower and reversed the switch. I mean, I was amazed and shocked.)

When I saw Mr Potts that particular morning all he could say was, 'They danced and sang!' 'Well, who?' I asked, 'Who danced and sang?' 'Those Elves,' he said, 'they danced and sang!' 'Yes,' he went on, 'they danced and sang.' 'You know what they said? They said humans are what they are and they must be accepted for what they are – some good , some bad, some very, very bad; others better, some much better, and others much better still, and a few are the best of the best. And the best thing of all? The best thing of all, they said, is that the best humans can give us grounds for hope,

hope that things will change for the better in time, the hope that the best will be victorious over the worst, so that in time, *in time* mind you, the world will be a much better place. Now, isn't that *some*thing?

The Elves had appeared to him in a dream, of course. And somehow they had given him something that smacked of hope. As I've already been at some pains to point out, hope was something he had abandoned long ago and now had been dragged to the surface, wet, bedraggled and forlorn, but still alive. Still alive and therefore to be accounted for, despite Mr Potts's fearful propensity to discount all forms of salvation for the human race.

I couldn't have done it. However many words I had employed, I knew I couldn't have brought about a turnaround in Mr Potts myself. The Elves had achieved it in a dream. But no, it was just too good to be true.

Of course! Nonsense! There could be no such thing! I knew that before Mr Potts had finished his second slice of toast he'd be his same old self – doubting, cynical and dismissive. And there'd be nothing either I or the Elves could do about it.

I was right, I'm afraid. 'But they'll need to do better than that! Oh, yes! Yes!' he said, with a wink and a nod while knocking back a second cup of tea, as though the cup and the tea inside it had let themselves down badly and irretrievably. 'Of course I know there are good things and bad things, beautiful things and ugly things – but there's just not enough of the good and the beautiful and far too much of the bad and the ugly, and that's not at all good enough for beings who pride themselves on being on a superior plane to that of the animals and, to boot, the creation of a loving god. There's a serious imbalance. And that's that! Oh, yes, they can dance and sing as much as they like, but facts are facts!'

'Well, things are as they are, and we can't do much about it,' I said, weakly, 'except be as decent as we can be ...' I must confess, after his outburst I didn't find my little contribution very convincing. Maybe he hadn't heard, or maybe he'd heard and found it even less convincing than I had – anyway, there was no response, and we both sat there quietly as though the subject of the human condition and of man's inhumanity to man hadn't been raised at all.

I thought about these things, but kept my thoughts to myself, for I knew very well that whatever came into my head had already been inside Mr Potts's head, where it had been carefully considered and given the attention it deserved. That gentleman Dostoyevsky had given such matters a lot of thought, and, somewhere in one of his books, he says, or he makes one of his characters say, that the world will be saved by beauty. I suppose what it means is that if, and it's a big if, the world is saved, it would be saved by beauty. And if what is meant is moral beauty, Mr Potts would probably have said that there just isn't enough of it to make a difference and that there never will be enough of it – so there! I know that Mr Potts was familiar with the ideas of Plato, because he'd quoted him often enough, especially where the philosopher says that the object of education is to teach us to love beauty. But when has education ever concerned itself with moral beauty as distinct from fitting the young for jobs, many of which they will spend the rest of their lives scorning and regretting? Mr Tolkien has one of his Elves say that the world is not all bad and that not all things are ugly and that things that are very bad, like wars and the grief they bring, can make good things like love grow the greater – yes, but this can't surely be an advertisement for war and grief, which we'd be infinitely better off without in the first place, or at least much better off with much less of it!

Well, anyway, I myself feel inclined to conclude with Mr Bunyan, in his *Pilgrim's Progress,* that we should be watchful and cast away fear, that we should be sober and hope to the end. (When he says 'sober', he doesn't mean that we should never drink to excess, although no doubt he would be one of the first to advocate sobriety. He means that we should be sensible and, I suppose, realistic. 'Realistic'! Oh, what a cumbrous word to carry round our necks!)

But here we touch once again upon Mr Potts's problem. He was definitely watchful and also fearless – but I'm not at all sure about his being realistic, and we know all too well that hope was a faded, dried-up flower in his lapel. Hope was a casualty of his having entertained moral possibilities for the human race that went far beyond the realm of what is achievable. As a massive and massively depressing counterweight to Mr Potts's speculations about the stupendous heights to which humans might aspire, was a passage he had copied and heavily underscored from some book he had been reading:

'*And we may think on this and perhaps profit from the debate, that the heights to which man may occasionally rise fall hopelessly short of the depths to which he sometimes sinks. On a vertical and volatile moral continuum, the descent of man is all too often infinitely and grotesquely faster than his ascent, which may well suggest a law of human nature the converse of which is yet to be satisfactorily proved.*'

I remember asking Mr Potts about the book. I forget the title, but it was, I seem to recall, written by a man called Brown – an apt name for such a dreary conclusion. My efforts to find the book amongst Mr Potts's effects has not proved successful, which is no doubt just as well. Anyway, Mr Potts clearly thought the passage summed up his own feelings, since it seemed to provide a bottomless pit for the alpine hopes he had erstwhile entertained.

Yes, it's plain to see. What Mr Potts needed was renewed hope, and faith that the things hoped for will come to be. And laughter, he needed that, too – but his humour was morose, his laughter cynical. I guess he had been held down by his own expectations, for when expectations far exceed possibilities, things like hope and faith hardly stand a chance. Sensing this, he'd abandoned his high expectations. But the heart of the problem is that he hadn't replaced them with expectations of a lesser, but still welcome, kind. Expectations of a lesser kind may seem reasonable if you believe with some people that human nature, far from being in a morally upward progression, is in fact in steady decline, the suggestion being that the more technology advances and the more people entrust themselves to it and become dependent upon it, the less they are capable of trusting one another and the more inward, that is to say selfish, they become, because technology tends to a most unwelcome form of isolationism, I mean the sort that physically separates people from each other. If so, moral expectations concerning human nature must be modified and revised downward – which is an interesting theory, but one exceedingly difficult to verify one way or the other. That being said, the theory has about it a surface validity when you consider how effectively social media, for example, functions as a channel of mutual abuse, and how efficiently computer technology lends itself to some of the basest forms of crime, not to mention the unthinkable avenues it offers for warfare on the greatest and most destructive of all possible scales.

Anyway, and downward spirals apart, in Mr Potts's world the baby had indeed been thrown out with the bathwater. And the hardest thing was how to restore some hope where there was none at all. A man without hope of any kind leads a vacuous, hollow sort of life, for, without hope, what is there for expectation to feed upon? Hope, for Mr Potts, withered on the vine from a diet lacking all nutrition.

(The phrase 'died on the vine' is not intended to evoke images of vineyards, bottles of Beaujolais or the raucous halls of Bacchus. Here it simply means that hope wasn't given a chance to grow, and died, as it were, in its infancy.)

If only something remarkable could have happened to restore some semblance of hope, and then perhaps some degree of feasible expectation!

But what on earth might it have been?!As I have I'm sure already mentioned, Mr Potts was not a religious man in any orthodox sense, if to be 'religious' it is necessary to believe in a god of some kind. It might have helped him, as it seems to help many others, if he could have brought himself to believe in a benevolent and loving God, one who would have assured him of a better life, albeit in some kind of Hereafter. Faced with the realities of the human condition, and particularly if he is of a most sensitive disposition, a man should never have to stand alone, and since we are all too often incapable of standing together, a benevolent God would have offered a most welcome reassurance that somehow, sometime, somewhere the bad will receive their just desserts and their victims full recompense, that evil will be confounded and good will prevail. Those who stand alone may begin to think fondly of death as some kind of release from the constant battering of their sensitivities and talk, like Keats, of 'easeful death' – sadly underplaying the fact that death will come whether we desire it or not, and is very likely to come when we desire it least. John Keats wrote that he was only 'half in love' with easeful death, no doubt sharing Andrew Marvell's speculation that, 'The grave's a fine and private place, But none I think do there embrace'. These lines were quoted by Mr Potts himself one morning when I found him in a pensive mood over breakfast. He didn't explain his thoughts, but I took it as a sure sign that thoughts of death were never far removed from his waking hours.

If Mr Potts had no faith in either God or man, he had given himself a hard time. It seemed like a waiting game, waiting for something cataclysmic to occur which would return him to the human fold and release him from his protective eccentricities. But it would necessarily have been something that kept the good in him intact, something that didn't transform him into the kind of human he despised so much, the kind he rejected, thinking it to be the template for the vast majority of the human race. But again, I was in the absurd position of wishing Mr Potts to change and still remain Mr Potts. Losing Mr Potts in the transformation would have been a tragedy – and of course I was painfully aware of this.

The Elves, despite the respect and admiration felt for them by Mr Potts, had, it seemed, failed to bring about a transformation in Mr Potts's attitude towards humans and the world in which they lived. Cynicism and despair had not been replaced, not even by a modicum of hope.

Chapter Thirteen

MR POTTS'S FEVER

Time passed as it invariably passes in stealth when people are stultified by routine and the everyday business of living, like a thief in the night when your house has been burgled and you are left with an acute sense of loss.

And then something happened, something very natural and you might even say 'normal' came about – some event, one which would normally have been taken very much for granted but which for Mr Potts turned out to be quite traumatic, as a small spark might cause a conflagration. Illness and disease are natural enough and hardly worth mentioning, unless, that is, they affect you personally or someone close to you and are of a most worrying kind.

Mr Potts fell worryingly ill. One unremarkable morning, toast and teacup fell out of his hands during a dizzy spell and he slumped to the floor, and the morning suddenly ceased to be unremarkable. I knelt over him and was relieved to find him conscious, though weak. I helped him to his chair, and then to his small bed which was thankfully on the ground floor in what he called his 'inner sanctum'. He looked so pale and spoke in whispers. He turned down any suggestion that a doctor or the emergency services should be called, which is what I'd have expected – his distrust of human nature easily extended to the medical fraternity and he was adamant that he would die with his boots on rather than in a hospital bed surrounded by strangers. His mention of dying was most upsetting and the thought flashed through my mind how poor the world would be without him, not to mention the effect on myself, since my affection for him had been steadily increasing despite the distance he had maintained, wittingly or otherwise, between himself and everyone else – and 'everyone else' included myself.

Even so, he was quite incapable of looking after himself. Whether his illness was the beginning of the end or just a temporary blip, he unquestionably needed someone to help him through it, and there was only myself on hand to do it. He signalled me away with a weak wave of his hand and then fell asleep. I decided to stay nevertheless, and took up temporary residence in the living room which adjoined the kitchen. Throughout the days that followed I peaked in on him, brought him tea and toast, having failed to persuade him to take something more nourishing, and did what I could to make him feel comfortable. I was a little surprised not to be waved away again – it was as though he accepted the fact that I should be there. Sometimes he seemed to be getting worse, sometimes better, but after about a week he began to perk up again by small degrees and it really did seem that he was on a slow mend – and so it turned out to be.

During one of those evenings when he seemed to drift in and out of sleep, he opened his eyes and asked me in a whisper, 'You're not one of *them* are you? Am I dreaming?' and then he drifted away again. I assume he was asking whether I was an Elf. In any case, it wasn't an answerable question and thankfully was only asked once, but Elves were referred to again. 'Why do you *bother?*' he asked, one very feverish evening, 'You must be ... an Elf!' – he raised his head a little from his pillow and then fell back into it again, none the wiser. Given how fondly Mr Potts had always spoken of the Elves and the virtuous powers he attributed to them, it's quite feasible to suppose that they are capable of stepping out of dreams to visit the sick and minister to them if, of course, they believe that a particular human is at all worth helping. But this is as much a subject for conjecture as anything else concerning those ethereal creatures, and I'll say no more about it. Since I am most definitely not myself one of them, I can only explain my motivation to help Mr Potts in very simple human terms. Which brings me to the old lady who lived at the bottom of a very long country lane.

This old lady, as eccentric as Mr Potts himself, though her eccentricities were expressed differently, consistently spoke about 'doing the loving thing'. There are, it must be said, those for whom the idea of doing the loving thing is nothing more than sentimental hogwash – these cynics would be the 'hard-headers' and 'hard hitters', the 'no-nonsense' fraternity amongst humans, those who cynically regard the do-gooders as 'softies'. Anyway, doing the loving thing is not easy in a world where the response to doing so is very often indifferent, negative or downright hostile. Doing the loving thing is so often regarded as an indication of weakness or of fear, because fear is almost invariably considered a weakness amongst humans. And then, when you're met with a negative response, the natural thing, if you're a typical sort of human, is to act negatively in return – it's probably because it's much easier to like someone who likes you than it is to like someone who dislikes you. But if you react negatively to a negative response, there seems to be no end to negativity, which might go on *ad infinitum*. Some humans have thought quite a lot about this and concluded that fear breeds fear, contempt breeds contempt, and so on. And this conclusion seems much safer than the contrary, that kindness breeds kindness. Of course, this is not to assert that kindness is incapable of breeding kindness, only that it doesn't seem to carry the kind of weight, the same degree of certainty, as the assertion that hate breeds hate. Naturally, Mr Potts would have gone much further than this – well, he would have gone further than this *before* his illness, but his illness seemed to have a profound effect on him. Which brings me to the traumatic nature of the whole event – something which, even now, I find hard to take in.

(A note may be advisable concerning the use of the word 'hogwash' here, which is not to be taken literally as meaning kitchen swill for pigs. It just means 'nonsense'. Even 'nonsense' does not really mean 'no sense', if it's thought to mean 'having no meaning whatsoever' – but that's another story. Also, the reference to 'hard headed' humans does not really mean that their heads are more physically impenetrable than other humans, any more than 'softies' should be taken to mean that some heads are softer to the touch than others. 'Hard headed' simply means obstinate and unkind, or somewhere between the two, as distinct from 'softie', which is a cynical reference to sensitivity and kindness. It's all getting a bit confused and confusing, I know, but one should be aware of how words are used, because, after all, words are all we have! For this reason, these short digressions are worthwhile – though, I agree, somewhat unsettling.)

Mr Potts's high fever eventually passed and he began to recover quite well, which meant that I needed only to drop in on him from time to time. It was during one of these drop-ins that I found him out of bed and in what was the middle, or possibly the end, of one of his speeches to an imaginary audience – not I think the Senate of ancient Rome, since, peeking through the keyhole of his bedroom door, I saw that he was not wearing one of his bath-towels in the manner of a toga over his pyjamas and was addressing ladies as well as gentlemen, and there were, as far as I know, no lady senators in ancient Rome, as they no doubt preferred to exercise their immense authority domestically, not caring whether men held sway in the corridors of power outside the home provided they were compliant inside it. And the wives of ancient Greece no doubt took a similar view. Accounts of Xanthippe, the wife of Socrates, preferring her husband's room than his company indoors and happy that he should pursue his philosophical inquiries outside in the market place are probably not at all entirely anecdotal.

Anyway, I dared not disturb Mr Potts in his speechmaking. Truth to say, I was delighted that at last he had enough energy for the task. I listened intently outside the door as he held forth in his customary eloquence (customary, that is, once he got going, like an old engine that becomes unstoppable on a downward track). I can't remember what he said word for word, but it went something like this:

' ... and what's more, ladies and gentlemen, I attribute it to the wisdom and generosity of my dreamlike bedfellows, I mean of course the Elves. I must confess my error, for in my youth I did expect far too much of humans. That was indeed a dream of quite another and very pleasing sort, but quite false. I did not realise how difficult the lives of humans are, and how hard it is for them to rise above their natures. Now I know better. But this realisation is not easy. When the thick and heady fog of pleasant illusion has thinned and lifted, the pain is not easy to bear, like a fever that weakens and debilitates the spirit. Now I know that most humans do their very best against fearful odds. There are amongst them those who would sooner be cast into fiery pits of oblivion than harm a fly – these perhaps we may call saints, and they are very few and far between, let me tell you. Then there are those who would think nothing of rendering the flesh and spilling the blood of the innocent and the good to achieve their ends – these we may call monsters. And then there are all those of differing degrees of imperfection, all of them knowing that their lives must come to an end while meanwhile they must suffer the intolerable grief of the loss of those who go before them. Humans are what they are and will be what they will be despite the faith that some have placed in what they call 'education', whatever form that education may take. I can feel nothing but sorrow and sympathy for them all. They live their short lives and then die, suffering the grief that is the price of love, and all they can do for one another is deck graves with flowers and shed tears. The good among the living do what they can against patently impossible odds, and they spend their poor lives attempting to make silk purses out of sows' ears. The deepest sympathy for the human lot is no more or less than what the Elves themselves feel – and this is what they have communicated to me, and I must suppose it is what they meant to communicate all along. In short, the human lot is not a happy one.

'Ladies and gentlemen, I repeat that the human lot is not a happy one, to put it politely and in deference to your sensitivities. And of all the things I could tell you now, I will say above all that each Christmas must be preserved and treasured, because, despite the battering Christmas has received and the attempt to reduce it to an orgy of spending and excess, it is one of the last opportunities remaining to bring humans to their senses, even if their sanity is short-lived – but better short-lived than deprived of life altogether! Christmas is a spring of hope, a reminder of how things should be and what, with greater effort and awareness, they *might* be. Never let the name of Christmas be altered, let alone removed from the calendar altogether. It is not one 'holiday' amongst others. It is not a holiday at all, although we might say that it offers an opportunity for a holiday from egoism and self-concern. Better to say that Christmas is a dream, a glorious dream, for it is not entirely false, even if it is not entirely true. We fall lamentably short of our dreams, but it would be immeasurably worse to stop having them altogether! It has been said that we should never ignore our dreams, that to do so is like refusing to read a letter addressed to ourselves. A dreamless sleep is not necessarily or always better than a sleep full of dreams. But the dream of Christmas is one that should never be ignored, for it's the very best of all dreams. The dream of Christmas is in the very word itself. And words are not *mere* words. No, they are vital! It is important which words we choose. A change of word is a change of sense, and the expulsion of a word is the destruction of the thing named. Christmas is Christmas, and let no one tell you otherwise. We must fight for our freedoms. But we must also fight for hope. Therefore, fight for Christmas! Kindness is in short supply. If you fight for Christmas you are fighting for kindness, fighting for love. And if anyone should say that the dream of Christmas is an impossible one, then I should say far better an impossible dream than no dream at all. In fact, impossible dreams may be the only dreams worth having, and I invite you to give this statement more than a passing glance in your considerations.'

(Be it duly noted that when Mr Potts spoke of making silk purses out of sows' ears, he was not lamenting the fact that pigs' ears are not the best material for making silk purses. He merely meant to say that attempts to improve the human condition fall far short of solutions.)

Then he went on:

'Ladies and gentlemen, I shall keep you no longer but will finish with this last and essential appeal, namely ... '

Perhaps this was to be his main thrust, one to which, however, I was not to be privy, since I was struggling to keep back a huge sneeze and the muffled sounds I was making outside the door must have been heard by Mr Potts himself. Anyway, he stopped just there and I was deprived of what was probably meant to be a spellbinding peroration. I have been kicking myself ever since for my inability to control my sneezing.

(I might say here, as it may go some way towards an apology, that I have always been subject to serious bouts of sneezing. One gigantic sneeze never seems adequate but is followed by four, five, six or even more, and during one fit of sneezing I counted ten! – each one louder than the other, which is why, once they start, I must make directly for a private place so as not to wake the dead or become a serious annoyance to the living. Mr Potts had experienced several of these unfortunate episodes, which of course served to distance us from one another, though, thank goodness, no irreparable, long-term harm was done to our relationship on account of my sneezing. I have heard it said that sneezing clears the head, though it leaves mine more confused than ever. Incidentally, when I say that I was 'kicking myself' I don't mean that I physically kicked one leg with the other in a masochistic bout of self-disapproval – apart from the physical difficulty in keeping this up for long, it would affect my ability to walk without bringing about a desirable result. I simply mean that I deeply regretted not hearing Mr Potts's last and 'essential appeal'.)

I was so struck by Mr Potts's sentiments that I backed away right out of the front door and made by way home, hoping that all along he had been unaware, or at least in sufficient doubt, of my presence. There was much to think about. Was it at all possible that Mr Potts had begun to believe in people again, even if with a thousand reservations? I was nonplussed and could reach no firm conclusion. I thought of asking him directly about it, but then he would know that I'd been listening in. No, I resolved simply to wait and see whether he would bring up the subject himself, if only tangentially, or whether he might say something that would give me the opportunity to make some kind of inroad into the whole subject. I was looking forward to our next tea and toast morning when something might be said. What did strike me was that his address to his imaginary audience was less like a speech and more like a sermon, and therefore what he imagined was less like an audience and more like a congregation. And sermons and congregations were not at all the kind of things Mr Potts formed attachments to. Perhaps, I thought, further light would be shed on this matter very soon.

I was to be disappointed. During the next tea and toast session we sat in silence for so long that I despaired of hearing one word, even the most casual and trite, from him – until, that is, he came out with a remarkable statement. 'It is not at all a pleasant thing for a good man to end his days in the certain knowledge that he is about to leave the world no better than he found it.' After such a long and disappointing silence, I was dumbstruck. I mean, it did sound like a perfect sentence, well articulated, and not like his usual staccato phrases addressed to no one in particular and machine-gunned into the air with no apparent beginning, middle or end. It reminded me at once of his latest outpourings. But I felt quite unable to respond to it – not there and then, at any rate. It was one of those statements that I had to take home with me and ruminate upon. I confess that I was, and still am, unable to take things in at once and respond appropriately, especially the kind of things Mr Potts habitually came out with. I put this down to my scant education, lack of experience and paucity of intellect. I am no match for Mr Potts, which is why I suspect he put up with me. Perhaps he pitied me for my lack of intellectual probity – I am guessing, of course, and dared not put the proposition to him. I usually felt like a weak Dr Watson to his highly perceptive Sherlock Holmes.

Anyway, as I sat there dumbstruck, he mumbled something about a suggestion he wanted to make to me but which had to wait until he felt that I and he himself were quite ready – 'And so, until we are ready then!' he barked. I took solace in an extra piece of toast, which I buttered slowly while still trying to get my head around the extraordinary statement he had just made and which was now followed by the idea that there was to be a 'suggestion' when the time was right.

Chapter Fourteen

MR POTTS IN LOVE

Truth to say, I have always been wary about suggestions when they are made by myself, and doubly cautious when they are made by other people. Suggestions are like moves in a game of chess played by amateurs, too often swift, badly thought out and ill-considered. And in the business of life and living, we are all amateurs. When Mr Potts finally came out with his promised suggestion, it seemed a glaring anti-climax. He proposed a day's walk in the countryside! 'Why?' I asked. 'We'll see,' is all he said.

We started out after tea and toast – first, a short drive, and then a long, winding walk down what was said to have once been a road built by the Romans for military purposes and which had now become a winding, leafy country lane over-hung on either side by overgrown branches of trees and bushes and wild shrubbery, and then we climbed up the rather steep, grassy incline of a hill. We stood on the flat top, surrounded by a panoramic view of the countryside around. 'This,' said Mr Potts, breathless from the climb, but more I suspect from excitement, '... this is what's left of an Iron Age fort. Do you see?' He pointed right and left to the undulations in the ground that marked the circumference of the fort. 'Built about 3,000 years ago, later attacked by the Romans, who killed just about everything that moved, and now ignored by everyone except archaeologists in occasional footnotes of passing interest. Why is it ignored? Because people say it's all in the past, and what's in the past, they believe, is of no relevance. 'Ahh, smell the air,' he said, taking a deep breath. 'It's the same air, is it not? The same as that breathed by the fort-dwellers! Can't you smell the smoke from their wood fires and the aroma of roasting meat? I tell you, it's the same. They say time moves on. I don't believe it! Time doesn't move anywhere – no, nowhere at all! Why? Because time doesn't exist! It's a figment of our imagination, a convenient and perverse device to prevent us from *thinking*. See?' I must have looked puzzled, and I was. 'Well ... no, I was afraid you wouldn't. Didn't I tell you the time has to be right? Well, the time isn't right. It's not right at all, and never will be!' Mr Potts spoke quickly. I had no chance to register what he was saying, let alone come up with a proper response; though, truth to tell, I'm not at all sure what a proper response would have been. I heard him say time didn't exist, but he was using the word. No wonder I looked puzzled, as anyone would when hit with a stark contradiction! I suppose I could have told him that what he was saying about time was just nonsense. I mean, how could he possibly say that time doesn't exist! We speak of time all the time, so how on earth could he say it doesn't exist? Yes, well, if anyone who'd called Mr Potts 'potty' could have heard him denying the existence of something that so obviously existed, they would consider their judgement regarding him perfectly justified – unless, of course, they believed he was suffering from a condition known throughout the ages as that of 'being a philosopher', an allowance which wouldn't really have let him off the hook, since philosophers are universally considered to be weak in the head and lacking in real practicalities. As for the air breathed by those ancient fort-dwellers being the same as the air we breathe now, I have no answer either way. I don't know how to measure sameness. But then, if you allow that time doesn't exist, sameness seems to make better sense. The mind boggles as much now as it did then, as it almost invariably did after Mr Potts's outpourings.

(I might here insert a note to the effect that when I say it wouldn't really have 'let him off the hook' I don't mean that Mr Potts was, is or ever would be caught on the end of a fishing line – I just mean that he would still be subject to criticism, or that his being a philosopher wouldn't have excused him from ignorant reproach. I'm almost sure my meaning is clear, but 'almost sure' is not the same as being certain, and, as you will no doubt appreciate, certainty is so often most helpful when it can be achieved – admittedly, there are circumstances where certainty is an extremely dangerous state of mind.)

'Many people, men, women and children died at the hands of the Romans here,' Mr Potts went on in a calmer, more pensive mood, as though talking to himself, 'They took no prisoners that day. They even slaughtered the animals. That was very wicked, wasn't it? Now, in answer to all those who say that it's all *in the past*, perhaps you can explain to me how I can hear their screams even now as we stand here, just as I can see their faces and the gleaming, blooded swords of their killers. So, you see, time doesn't exist. People say, what's done is done. But I say, what *has been* done *is being* done, right now, yes, *in the here and now!*' He spoke in a rising crescendo and this last sentence burst upon the air like a gunshot.

Then, after a few moments silence, Mr Potts viewed the countryside from the top of the hill and remarked upon its beauty, calmly, pensively and as though thinking out loud. 'Strange, isn't it, how so much that is bad can co-exist with such beauty as this, like a cruel play acted out on a beautiful stage?' 'Yes, it's beautiful! How can anyone who sees such beauty wish for death - his own or anyone else's? Makes me wish I could see and touch as well as hear all those who died here and attempt some kind of apology for the mess that human nature is. Come on, let's get out of here!' With that, which was the last thing he said to me that day, he began the descent, beckoning me to follow.

Well, that experience was short-lived but unforgettable – though I still have difficulty fully understanding its significance. Maybe Mr Potts really had lost his senses. Yet, something had changed. Something in our relationship, perhaps. Why did he want *me* to see the remains of the fort on the hill? I mean, why bother, unless it *meant* something to him that *I myself* should see it and maybe learn something from it? Was I now a friend and not just someone to eat toast and drink tea with? Was the whole episode a sign that there was to be a change in our relationship – that somehow I was to be trusted in a way in which I hadn't been before? I felt like a student on graduation day – evidently not top of the class, but not at the bottom, either. Yes, but the whole episode was mind-boggling and I couldn't make sense of it.

In fact, it kept me awake all night as I tried to figure it all out. As for his denial that time existed, it seemed on the face of it perverse and absurd. Religious people would appeal to the authority of Scripture to contradict him flatly. After all, isn't it said in *Ecclesiastes* (3: 1-8 to be precise) that there's a time for everything, a time for every purpose under heaven: a time to be born, a time to die, a time of love, a time of hate – well, I can't remember them all, but there's quite a few things that are given a time there. But then I thought that maybe he wasn't denying the existence of time at all.Maybe it was just his way of saying that people don't change – the good, the bad, the beautiful, the ugly, the fat, the thin, the wise, the cruel, the kind and the stupid never change, and so it follows that what they *do* doesn't change, either. Maybe denying the existence of time was another way of saying that history repeats itself over and over, that the same play with the same characters is repeated over and over though the set may change. And, in any case, why bother to make the point? What did it all come to?

And then it seemed to follow that the whole thing wasn't about *me* at all, at least certainly not *all* about me. I was just a witness, though I felt strangely ennobled to have been chosen – but chosen to witness *what*? Maybe I had been chosen to witness an act of love! Yes, it struck me that Mr Potts was in love – in love with the world after all and therefore bitterly critical of all those things that upset the applecart of life and love. But I had a strange and uncomfortable feeling that I was myself in danger of contracting the disease of philosophy with all these mental meanderings. I mean, it was much easier to say that Mr Potts was insane and leave it at that! Yes, calling people crazy and leaving it at that is a temptation difficult, if not impossible, to resist, especially if you're not up to the business of thinking about things for more than a minute and a half, and, sad to say, the vast majority of humans stupidly consider that a full 90 seconds is more than enough to make a contribution to the corpus of what they perceive to be idle philosophical speculation. Oh! what can be done about human stupidity? Alas, alack, very little, I fear.

(Allow me to point out that the expression 'to upset the applecart' is not a reference to apples or, indeed, to fruit of any kind, and nor is it a reference to their mode of transportation. The expression simply means 'to cause harm or trouble gratuitously'. This figurative mention of carts is reminiscent of one of Aesop's fables: Hermes was driving all over the world with a cartload of lies, deceit and wickedness, distributing a little of the contents in each country – until he came to one country in particular where the cart irretrievably broke down spilling its contents on the ground, where it was keenly retrieved by the inhabitants thinking it to be of great value. Aesop courageously identifies which country this was, but I, in deference to the sensitivities that Mr Potts would expect of me, do not.)

If Mr Potts was rightly judged to be insane, it seems to follow that those who judged him to be so are themselves quite *sane*! Well, the wilderness in which we live is full of thorny thickets, one in which the judges are deemed to be beyond judgement and those who are subject to judgement are perceived to be rightly and justly judged. If we believe Plato, and I think we are pleasantly constrained to do so, Socrates was himself judging his judges at his trial. Who will be wise enough and brave enough to judge the judges? I must confess, I am bewildered. Poor Mr Potts! Would no one judge in his favour? And who other than Socrates himself would judge the judges who judged against him? He stumbled in the darkness of his times, and it's only right and proper that a wise man should stumble. Those who walk with confidence through the darkness of their times are either saints, whose number is minuscule and whose courage is taken for granted, or sinners, and, if the latter, the darkness through which they walk is of their very own creation. Yes, poor Mr Potts! – forever to be spoken down and considered inferior to the vast bulk of mankind.

From the hilltops of the Iron Age fort, he saw the beginning, the middle and the end of the world. Well, how many can claim such a vision? I saw nothing of the sort, but that's because I'm not Mr Potts and could never be like him. I see only what lies ahead in the routine of the next day. If I could see with clarity further than that, I might not be capable of holding on to what most humans call 'sanity'.Mr Potts was in danger of transmuting me into a philosopher – or a philosopher of sorts. He had, if only tangentially and to a lesser extent than he would have wanted, encouraged me to think in stranger ways. He had encouraged me to question and to wonder, and in so doing he had helped to estrange me from the world of the common man without at the same time my becoming either more or less than the common man – but he had estranged me from the common man who thinks only of the things he is told to think about, and preferably only of the things that matter on the morrow, like getting up in time for work, of not upsetting the boss, of keeping time with the rest of humanity and of expecting and desiring those things that the rest of mankind expects and desires. For this reason, Mr Potts was really an exceedingly dangerous individual, for he encouraged me to step outside the goldfish bowl of life and all who swim in it and to observe it as from 'outside', while at the same time I swim 'inside' it and am subject to all its follies – a precarious and not altogether pleasant experience, rather like a mortgage that you can never really pay off. It's rather like the mathematician who is also a philosopher – one foot in, one foot out.

As I believe I've said already, things tended to come in bits from Mr Potts, like the pieces of a jigsaw. They were given sparingly and had to be waited for. And, like jigsaw pieces, some were more revealing than others.

One morning following the Iron Fort expedition, he exclaimed, 'Yes, I've a very great deal to thank the Elves for.' He then went on to elaborate, and, knowing Mr Potts, elaboration was not at all what I expected. 'Yes, I really believe they've plucked me from the depths of depression like a fish from deep waters. People of a religious disposition might say that depression is wicked because it makes you blind to the goodness that exists and turns you into a cynical beast. Of course, they don't mean that depressed people are wicked. On the contrary. They mean that depression is the work of the devil, because a denial of goodness is precisely what the devil wants from you. Well, the Elves have taught me to understand this! In doing so, they've given me a very great gift. Yet, I've done nothing for *them*, given them *nothing*. They've taught me that humans have so much to put up with, that being a human creature is *hard*, yes, *very* hard – and that's why they, the Elves, must suffer, too! If only humans could be better than they are, they'd do the Elves a tremendous favour! If only humans could let their imaginations run free in a happier world!' Then he returned to the business in hand - buttering another piece of toast.

(It struck me as rather odd that he should have mentioned the devil. You would have thought it strange for a man who was not at all religious. After all, if you believe in the devil, it would seem to imply a belief in God. But then there's a difference between 'Devil' with a capital letter and 'devil' without – and I assumed he meant the latter, so that he was talking figuratively, as it were. Don't we say things like, 'What the devil is he doing!'? Even so, I was somewhat taken aback.)

Thinking about what he had said, it occurred to me that Mr Potts had indeed given the Elves *something*. He'd given them grounds for hoping that there might be more humans like Mr Potts, because if there were more like him the world would be a decidedly better place and at last the existence of Elves would be universally and unquestionably acknowledged and, more than this, they'd be given the respect they so richly deserved.

What the Elves were up to, if they were up to anything at all, and what they had in mind I can't for the life of me tell. But there was certainly a change in Mr Potts, discernible but subtle, subtle but discernible. He had once lamented the use of the word 'love', which, he said, was ironically in very common usage since it could only be properly applied comparatively rarely. He had avoided using the word, and I was not surprised that he still did. But now he seemed less cynical in his observations. Now he seemed to love the very great majority of humans for their very *weaknesses* rather than, as before, the small minority for their great strengths. He had come to see that being a human is not at all an easy condition to have to live with. And this seemed to me an expression of love.

As an instance of this, as I walked up the garden path and approached the front door on one of our regular tea and toast mornings, I found him in the doorway with arms outstretched and upward, as though he were greeting a dear old friend after a long, not to say painful, absence. I was mistaken. He had something else in mind and was, as they say, making a point.

'You see,' he exclaimed, 'this is all you can do! All you can do is throw up your arms and let things be what they are!' We went inside and sat at the table. 'My point is obvious, is it not? It's a question of control, and of change. There are some things you can control and some things you can change. But when it comes to the human condition, you're quite stuck! There's precious little you or anyone else can do about it, and that's that! All you can do is throw your arms into the air and admit as much, even before the battle has been joined. There can be no battle because there's only one army and that army is arrayed *against* you. Perhaps we should be grateful we can't control or change the human condition. Humans are stuck with what they are – occasional lights in a dark landscape. And what cold, dark places await them in their declining years! Places where the silences can never be broken by the banging of doors or the jangling of jailers' keys. Places in which it's too late for either hate or love. Poor, poor creatures, I really do feel so very sorry for them. Well, well, that's how it is!' he said, as he jumped up from the table and shot up his arms once more, narrowly missing the rather pendulous light shade en route.

Ever since that morning I can't think of Mr Potts without that image – shooting his arms up into the air and shouting, 'Let it be! Let it be!' And once again I had a confusion of ideas to disentangle and have not managed it to this day. But it was, I concluded, evidence of some kind of acceptance of the weaknesses of fellow humans. Was it an acceptance of his own weaknesses as well? Yet he continued to think of himself as quite different from the common run of humans. It was barely days after the 'Let it be!' incident that I heard him addressing a rather large marrow in his vegetable plot with the words, 'I've prided myself on being different, so if you expect me to be like all the rest of them, you're very much mistaken. It's just not on! And I expect the same from *you*!' I assumed that by 'them' he meant humans, not marrows, and by 'you' he meant the marrow, and that he was simply thinking out loud and not actually responding to an enquiry made by the marrow in question – to assume otherwise would be rather silly, for even Mr Potts, as potty as he might indeed have been, would be unlikely to mistake a marrow for a human being, though humans themselves have been known to make mistakes easily as ludicrous.

Chapter Fifteen

ENLIGHTENING CONTRADICTIONS

If – and here I am just speculating as usual – if Mr Potts had become less cynical and more embracing of human weaknesses, might it not be that his expectations of human capabilities had also become less strict or demanding? Well, the situation is not at all clear, as the forgoing chapters should indicate. He was a man of constant ambivalence, if I may put it like this – forever blowing hot and cold, as it were. He seemed able to admit of human frailties, yet at the same time he refused to contemplate the idea that he was himself a member of the human race. He might only have agreed that he was and was not human. A most disagreeable contradiction! Contradictions are most unwelcome in human logic, though it seems the Elves allow them more readily.

Then again, if he sympathised with humans on account of their weaknesses, going so far as to grieve on their behalf, wouldn't it have followed that his expectations of them, once so high and mighty, should have been lowered proportionately?

He was, in fact, quite incapable of throwing the whole matter over his shoulders, incapable of leaving the human condition where it is and where it has always been and where no doubt it always will be. Humour might have helped, but he seemed devoid of humour. I mean, the greatest comedians are those who despair the most – or so it might seem, their humour being a kind of balm for what they see as an extremely troubled world. The joy of life should be shared, and the greatest comedians, being great-hearted, can't abide the fact that there are humans hell-bent on depriving the joy of life to other humans.

(When I say 'he was incapable of throwing the whole matter over his shoulders', I am not, of course, referring to Mr Potts's lack of acrobatic abilities or his muscular deficiencies. I simply mean that he was *incapable of ignoring* the human condition. Similarly, when I say Mr Potts was 'forever blowing hot and cold', I am not inviting you to picture him as a boiler in the act of adjusting itself. The expression simply means that his moods were extremely changeable, as when someone is enthusiastic one moment and downcast or indifferent the next.)

If there is ample reason to despair, what's the use of it if the majority can't feel it – can't *feel the same way*? If enough people felt despair, they might be motivated to change the world for the better. For despair is most distressing and can't be tolerated for long. They would either be motivated to change the world or to leave it!

But these idle thoughts are mine alone. I couldn't have shared them with Mr Potts. Mr Potts was a man who stood alone. He was a man who knew his own mind, insofar as it is ever possible for anyone to know their own mind.

('Knowing your own mind' is not to be confused with 'Knowing yourself'. 'Know yourself', a stricture handed down by the ancient Greeks, seems doable if said quickly enough but becomes a gargantuan task when properly acted upon – so much so that it's to be wondered whether anyone can actually succeed in doing it. However, any human worried about the difficulty of knowing himself may rest assured that no one else has yet succeeded and that he is in all probability the only human even barely contemplating the task. Moreover, If knowing yourself is so hard, what are we to say about knowing *another*?)

Of course, if we say that Mr Potts was a changed man, this isn't to say that he was essentially different. The fact that the Iron Age fort was built on a hilltop was essential to the security of the inhabitants. In like manner, Mr Potts insisted that a person of integrity should occupy a place on a mountain top and strive to remain there against all the odds.

(Naturally, I'm speaking figuratively, for life on a real mountain top is not at all conducive to good health and comfort and is not the right kind of example to set for those wishing to settle down and start a family. It's really a way of speaking about the importance of maintaining moral integrity and a degree of calm detachment in a world which too often either undervalues them or ignores them altogether.)

Some contradictions are worthy of note and perhaps not a little respect. For a person of uncommon integrity may be both in *and* out of this world. He sees the world as though he were looking into a goldfish bowl and doesn't truly feel part of it. Would it be possible to feel like this on drugs, as though it were a kind of permanent high? But if drugs have anything to do with it, it must be fake and bears no relation to moral integrity, which is a painfully sober sort of thing. Drugs in themselves may produce feelings of intense elation and moral detachment. Integrity, in itself, does not.

I've had it on the best authority, I mean from Mr Potts himself, that when you're brought low with self-doubt, it's all too easy to persuade yourself or to be persuaded by others that your place on the mountain top is undeserved and that you should climb down to the murky depths below and join the fray. In moments of weakness, and such moments are common enough, you might begin to doubt your own judgements and principles, for it's much easier to play the games that others play than it is to question them – rather like the trick played on the man who was made to doubt his judgement about the colour of a thing when everyone else in the room falsely declared that he was wrong. 'You've just got to keep on track, hard though it may be. Stick to the straight and narrow!' Mr Potts would insist.

He made the point in other ways, just in case I hadn't grasped it the first time. He said you had to be like a fixed point on the circumference of a circle when everyone else is running all round it. Sooner or later, they'll all come back to you, if they keep moving at all. The man who is unrepentant in his convictions during a frenzy of change will one day be vindicated. Or, he said, it's like a man who refuses to dress according to the latest fashions but stays with the tried and tested – sooner or later, when the crazes have all burnt out, he'll be revered as a paradigm of plain common sense.

Of course, it's not enough just to have any old convictions. They have to be *right* as well.But that opens a Pandora's box of issues, a philosophical labyrinth which I'm not competent to deal with. When he was kind enough to enquire, I told Mr Potts he'd made his point quite clear and I thanked him for it. But when I got home I realised I hadn't understood a thing, except that you had to try to be true to yourself – I think I understood that, but, then again, these things are quite foggy.

(When he spoke of 'track' and 'the straight and narrow', Mr Potts wasn't really talking about railways lines or jungle pathways. He meant that you have to keep faith with yourself, know what your principles are and maintain them. He might have said instead that you must 'stick to your guns', meaning much the same thing, for this is not a reference to field artillery and being glued to a field gun.)

Of course, there will always be someone who will argue that it's not at all easy to know what your principles are, let alone stick to them, just as it isn't easy to know yourself – well, no doubt there's a point or two here worth pursuing, but not myself being up to the task of giving them the kind of philosophical analysis that Mr Potts is capable of giving them, all I can do is to acknowledge them and leave them at that. I might add that if we find it hard to know our limits in the innumerable bars that populate the globe, it's little wonder that we should find it even harder to know ourselves! Is 'knowing yourself' just knowing what your principles are and perhaps reminding yourself of what you know – if so, I think humans are all in with a chance of knowing themselves or, at least, knowing themselves much better.

So, there we are. The mellowing change that seemed to have come over Mr Potts was not one that could shake his integrity. It was one, rather, that admitted the difficulty of being a human in a world of humans. And this, above all, included the difficulty of getting other humans to see things as you do and to share your moral indignation, especially when you are utterly convinced that the way you see them is unquestionably right. You can go on stating what for you is obvious right and proper, only to be met with a wall of silence or with arguments that seem to you either too weak for words or besides the point altogether – as though the words used against you were leaves that blew away in the wind without so much as 'touching base' *en route* (to use an expression from the game of baseball – a mere game, but the immense value of which, like that of football, is universally and unequivocally agreed upon).

The gist of what I understood to be Mr Potts's position was this, that although the animal in even the best of humans was never too far from the surface, this was something for which they could not be blamed. Those who, despite everything, still cling to the notion of a Benevolent Creator, might call it, for want of a less lazy and more enlightened description, a 'structural defect' in their natures, but one for which they cannot themselves be held responsible. In short, humans need to wage a perpetual battle against such a 'defect', with varying degrees of commitment and success, which is what had earned the sympathy of Mr Potts. On the geological scale, the expression 'Civilised man' must therefore always be written in inverted commas as far as Mr Potts was concerned, though it seems to me that we should be most thankful that man is not even less civilised than he is. Mr Potts's position does, however, allow a few tears to be shed for the fearful odds mankind is up against – odds the source of which lies deep within him.

To rephrase the matter in terms that the more mystical among humans might appreciate, but which Mr Potts wouldn't himself have chosen: it is indeed true that the spirit of man is willing but his flesh is weak – but he is not to be blamed for that!

Chapter Sixteen

THE GLADIUS AND THE SPEAR

For some years after Mr Potts's more 'mellowed' (if I may use the word) critique of humans, I continued to visit him for tea and toast two or three times a week, fascinated as I was to discover and record the change that I felt sure to have detected in him, but detected 'as through a glass darkly', since he was, if anything, less forthcoming than ever before in his staccato pronouncements.

As time went by, I noticed that there was no mention of the Elves, and I was determined to test whether they were still an important item in Mr Potts's world, or whether they were any longer an item at all. Finally, I decided to broach the subject by asking, 'Do you sleep well, these days? You look a bit peaky.' 'I'm perfectly fine,' he said. 'I sleep like a log, a very heavy log.' 'No, intervention from the Elves, then?' 'None,' he replied. 'They've done their job. I daresay they're around to keep me on the right track – they're quiet and waiting, for now!' I'm not sure whether I was disturbed or relieved to hear this. Anyway, there was no hint of irony or humour in his voice. He was, as usual, quite matter-of-fact. I decided to make no further reference to the Elves unless and until I was invited to do so.

(I interject the note that when Mr Potts said that he slept like a log, we are not to suppose that a log actually sleeps. To do so would be considered as silly as supposing that it might awaken if you shouted at it or tripped over it. But logs lie motionless until moved, and the idea of sleeping *like* a log means that you sleep soundly and undisturbed. The general rule is that only sentient beings can sleep or wake, and sentient beings are thought to properly comprise animals of all sorts and humans. A sentient being is one that has the power of perception by or through the senses of hearing, taste, touch, hearing and sight, though no doubt the Elves themselves would wish to attribute such power to the kingdoms of plants, mountains, lakes, seas, rivers and even stones – and certainly logs. But logs are, at least by humans, considered to be insentient on account of their being dead things. Alas, alack, human imagination is a poor thing, heavily weighted on the side of the grotesque and the intolerably heinous – a fact that causes much discomfort and regret amongst the Elves, who would wish it to be infinitely richer than it is. Native Americans were much closer to the Elves than most other humans, since all things animate or otherwise were regarded as their relatives – I say 'were' because I'm not at all sure that they still are! Anyway, for their depth and breadth of imagination, Elves regard Native Americans as fondly as we do our loved ones – or so Mr Potts said when, on one of his extraordinary birthdays, he waxed lyrical about what he called the 'magic' of imagination and went on to lament bitterly its gradual decline, and went so far as to predict its eventual disappearance amongst humans.)

Mr Potts's more kindly attitude towards humans proved to be a very fickle thing – which accorded perfectly with what I knew all along about his ambivalence. When I dared mention a disturbing item in the news, which I thought should be aired, Mr Potts forgot himself in a burst of anger and indignation. I had momentarily forgotten that I should keep human affairs to myself. But it was a kind of test case. He was most indignant. 'Idiots!' he shouted, thumping the table hard, causing teapot, toast rack and butter dish to leap towards the ceiling and fall back again somewhat worse for wear.

What this episode clearly demonstrated was that his deeper sympathies for creatures saddled with human nature were quite compatible with his stark condemnation of their unbridled proclivities towards wickedness and their pursuit of purely selfish ambitions at the expense of others.

(Allow me to point out, quite unnecessarily I'm sure, that my use of the words 'saddled' and 'unbridled' are not meant to refer literally to horses. They are figurative expressions connoting, as you know, 'possession' and 'lack of control' respectively. But then, come to think of it, horses are quite like humans in this context. You might well sympathise with horses which are obliged to wear saddles, especially if you are a bare-back rider like the Native Americans of old, but you would not wish to excuse them for kicking the life out of their riders in protest.)

To come back to Mr Potts, my considered conclusion from the above episode was that he was not yet ready, and I feared might never be so, to return to the vast community of humans into which he was born and in which he was suckled. Despite the many instances of self-sacrificial love that might be encountered daily, despite the language of true love that is, though increasingly thin, still extant and to be met with in birthday and Christmas cards and the like, Mr Potts was so overwhelmed at the thought of human cruelties that were at least equally common as professions of love and affection that he felt too uncomfortable with his own kind to feel at home with them. And so, the best that could be said of him is that he was probably half-human. The other half remained with the Elves that he could only dimly perceive in his dreams and perhaps in the slippery shadows of the twilight hours. Despite his sympathies, Mr Potts was not to be persuaded as to the essential or inevitable beneficence of the human race.

Of course, Mr Potts's position seemed to me quite unenviable. I suppose it was inevitably uncomfortable, as anyone will tell you who has stood with one foot in the river and the other on the riverbank – which is not a posture that anyone in his right senses wishes to adopt if he has any reasonable choice in the matter.

(Of course, we're not concerned here with real rivers and riverbanks. The whole point is that it's hard to belong to two camps which are diametrically opposed to one another.)

Mr Potts was neither one thing or the other – neither human nor Elf. Even if he had wanted to place both feet in one camp, he was not allowed to do so. Humans rejected him because they considered him irredeemably potty. Elves wouldn't have him because no human could ever become an Elf no matter how hard he tried. The irony of it is, and here I am of course speculating as usual, that Mr Potts, or anyone else for that matter, wouldn't in any case have been entirely happy to become wholly an Elf, just as Mr Potts wasn't entirely happy to be wholly human. Mr Potts was therefore stuck with being neither here nor there.

The trouble, some clever humans might say, with his being neither here nor there is that he was nowhere at all – a conclusion that *follows*, some might say. But Mr Potts is a clear example of someone who was definitely *somewhere*. You might even go so far as to say that 'nowhere', contrary to popular opinion, is indeed a place, and a very significant place at that. It's rather like someone saying, 'He'll get nowhere if he goes on like that', or 'She got nowhere in life' – and things like this are supposed to be criticisms or reproaches. But I'm of the firm conviction that nowhere may be a most desirable place to be, which is not at all the same as saying that it's a comfortable or pleasant place to be. Yet, someone who finds himself in the middle of nowhere may find himself in the best possible place. Of course, not having the analytical tools that were enjoyed by Mr Potts I can't be sure what I mean by what I say or that I am saying what I really mean – a state of affairs not at all uncommon amongst the human race. Our thoughts can be quite roguish by allowing themselves to be expressed by words that don't properly convey them.

And this brings me to another unforgettable breakfast-time 'conversation' with Mr Potts, one of those episodes in which he became vociferous in one of those rare and flowing tirades.

I happened to remark on one of those historical events which illustrates man's inhumanity to man by innocently saying, 'It just doesn't make sense!'

'What's that!' said Mr Potts, his slice of toast halted between plate and mouth as though frozen in ambling flight. 'But it makes *perfect* sense! It's what humans *are* after all! Doing evil, being wicked, is a thoroughly *human* skill. No, what you mean to say is that it is most disagreeable. You want to mean that you find it morally distasteful and unacceptable, *bestial* even – and I quite agree. But what you want to mean is not what you are actually *saying*. Because human failings make perfect *sense*. You should be more careful with your use of words. Words are all we have – I'm sure I've said that before. You're slipping. A temporary lapse, I trust.' With that, his slice of toast finally found its mark.

Mr Potts, a stickler for verbal precision, was ticking me off. But he hadn't finished. He later went on at unprecedented and alarming length, 'This imprecision of yours is a thoroughly *human* trait, of course. And that's how you learned it. Precision is wasted on humans, anyway, as I'm sure you've noticed. Humans listen without hearing, one of their greatest faults. They come to something with a fixed and immovable prejudice which blinds them to the possibility of effective alternatives and precision goes out the window – if it was there in the first place, which I very much doubt. You need only look at the internecine doings in their House of Commons – once they find an angle in a member of the Government or the Opposition they go for it unto death, all objectivity is cast aside, the aim being simply and solely to bring someone down and if they can do so by public humiliation they consider it the cherry on the cake. Once their claws are in they will not let go until their victim is cut into pieces, and they are not averse to kicking a man once he is down. They may think themselves very clever, but all they show is toxicity and hate, which are anything but the hallmarks of beneficent leadership. For this, so-called politicians earn for themselves only the disrespect of the wise and the tears of a benevolent God. The fate of Socrates was nothing extraordinary but simply one case amongst an infinity of grave injustices and internecine doings all masquerading as acts of public decency and duty. Here you can see clearly that humans are wolves with human heads. Slogans replace precision, prejudice trumps objectivity, and the gloves are off!Now what are we to call such creatures? Are they wolves with human heads? Or shall we say they are humans with wolfish dispositions? Or, as I prefer, should we simply call them *human*?They are frequently at war with one another, and if there is a risk of peace they *simulate* war, or they wage a *cold* war, and in the temporary absence of all war, they butcher each other with words – for words replace the gladius and the spear of the gladiatorial ring. Precision requires thought and judgement, and thought and judgement in turn require ...'

Here Mr Potts suddenly broke off, as though he himself couldn't find the right words to satisfy his tireless and ruthless demand for verbal precision.

(Let me just quickly point out that Mr Potts's reference to 'the cherry on the cake' is not meant to be a culinary observation, much less a suggestion for a recipe. He meant that, amongst humans, humiliation of an opponent is a 'welcome bonus'. Likewise, the phrase 'cold war' does not connote a war in winter or in the colder regions of the planet – it simply refers to a figurative war of attitudes in relation perhaps to opposing ideologies and a consequent indisposition to compromise amicably.)

In any case, I felt I had been soundly reprimanded for betraying a human weakness, namely a lazy use of words. The effect, however, was to make me even more hesitant to say anything at all in Mr Potts's presence lest I should incur his wrath again. Instead, words were, as often as possible, replaced by facial expressions in response to what Mr Potts himself actually said. I tried to adopt the habit of frowning, smiling and twisting my face into all kinds of contortions merely to express an appropriate response to what I believed Mr Potts was expressing – approval, mainly disapproval, surprise, shock, horror, disbelief, and so on.

My tendency to resort to facial contortions didn't, however, last very long. They were phased out after Mr Potts accused me of developing ticks and twitches and suggested that I should seek a medical consultation as a matter of some urgency. After that, I tended to confine my responses to single words and phrases as a result of which I felt convinced that I was turning into Mr Potts himself, since these were his more customary modes of expression. Despite my acute admiration for him, the very prospect of becoming another Mr Potts failed to excite me. I resolved instead to improve verbal precision and, though I say so myself, I believe I made noticeable progress, though I still tried hard to limit the frequency and the length of my own verbal outpourings. In any case, Mr Potts never again, as far as I can recollect, reprimanded me for linguistic confusion or paucity of expression.

Chapter Seventeen

MR POTTS – NEITHER HERE NOR THERE

I hadn't paid Mr Potts a visit for at least a fortnight when I received some shocking, indeed heart-rending, news.

Mr Potts had met his end in a prosaic manner quite unbefitting his eccentric stature, at least that's how it seemed to me. An eye-witness described how, without a care in the world, he stepped off a double-decker bus while whistling to himself and began to cross the road, only to be hit by a car that was exceeding the speed limit. His death was said to have been instantaneous. 'He wasn't looking where he was going!' the eye-witness said, and that's *all* that was said. Case closed. His life had ended in an instant, not so much as a single flash of glory. It seemed far too simple and unsatisfactory, like a mere full-stop to round off an extraordinarily good sentence – though, I must hasten to add, without a full-stop it would not be a 'sentence' at all!

I heard about the tragedy during a phone call from a lawyer who said that I had inherited Mr Potts's house under the terms of his will. He asked whether I wanted to attend the funeral, which, he said, he had been instructed to arrange and pay for. 'I represent the deceased,' said the lawyer. It surprised me at first to hear these words – how could anyone even begin to *represent* Mr Potts! Mr Potts had mistrusted just about everyone, but I suppose legal necessity obliged him to hire a lawyer.

I could hardly believe it. I had thought Mr Potts to be quite indestructible. He had, I thought, every right to live forever and, with the Elves to support him, might well have done so. On second thoughts, I knew it would have been rather cruel to have wished eternal life on the poor fellow. Tea and toast would surely lose their attraction eventually. As it was, all those toast and tea mornings we enjoyed together suddenly seemed to come to nothing. I found myself absurdly wondering whether the Elves had sanctioned his demise and even brought it about. Then I thought the Elves wouldn't have wanted him gone – but couldn't they have prevented his demise if they have the powers Mr Potts was fond of attributing to them? And then I wondered why he had taken that bus ride. He wasn't one to leave the house except to do a bit of local shopping for essentials. The circumstances of his demise, the whys and wherefores of it all, were fast taking on the character of a whodunit. I thought there *must* be something behind it.

But then I remembered what Mr Potts used to say about the word 'must', it being the kind of word that can lead us into all sorts of byways and cause a great deal of confused thinking, leading us into blind alleys and driving us to despair, for behind it is the conviction that nothing can be what it seems, that there *must* be something behind everything. 'It's a human weakness,' I remember him saying, 'It's a disease of the human mind. It's a refusal to take things at face value when all they have is face value. Of course, not everything should be taken at face value, but because of this humans begin to think that *nothing* should be taken at face value, and this gets them into all sorts of trouble, you see? Humans butcher logic, like a surgeon who uses the right scalpel but makes the wrong incision!'

Yes, that's something I shall never forget – 'the right *scalpel*, the wrong *incision*'. Well, anyway, it took some time before I could accept the simplicity of the circumstances surrounding Mr Potts's departure from the world of humans. After making some straightforward enquires, I discovered that Mr Potts had been carrying a bag of mixed fruit. Clearly enough, he'd gone to the grocer in the next village to get them because he had always refused point-blank to buy them from the superstore ever since that very unfortunate incident which I believe I have already been at pains to recount. There was no 'whodunit' after all, and Mr Potts's strictures about the cavalier use of the word 'must' had been proved right. As for his not looking where he was going, I would have expected nothing else – his head was always full of everything except the simplest of matters in hand. I continued to wonder, though, whether he had departed that world and entered the realm of the Elves. I continued to wonder because I suppose I wanted very much for it to be so. I couldn't get my head round his being non-existent and wanted life for him, some sort of life and preferably a much better one than he had known.

I attended the funeral, of course – how could I not? I thought it an extremely sad affair, but then I knew it was also the most fitting for Mr Potts. Sad, because I was the sole mourner. Sad, also, because the officiating priest simply mouthed the usual perfunctory clichés. And that was that. I might have tried to say a few words myself – but to *whom*? And so, there was no 'service' as such. Mr Potts's remains were turned into ashes, and his ashes were turned over to me in the absence of contactable relatives. Fitting, because, from what I knew of him and in view of the arrangements he had himself made, the whole business would have been regarded by him to be no more than the practical, efficient and respectful disposal of his remains – no trimmings, no saintly speeches, no weeping mourners, and therefore the risk of hypocrisy was by and large eliminated. And since all expenses were defrayed to the last penny, there was nothing for me to do but attend and then leave with Mr Potts entombed in a small ceramic jar, and his house keys in my pocket.

I made directly for his house, which I had already decided to keep and reside in. After selling my own house, I would live in the house he had left me – which is precisely what happened. I placed Mr Potts's pot (meaning the pot that contained his ashes) on a shelf of the Welsh kitchen dresser overlooking the breakfast table. I decided to continue the tea and toast mornings as though he were still in the land of the living. In a sense, of course, he's still very much in the land of the living – I mean his *ashes* are. I also routinely set the breakfast table for two and make enough tea and toast for both of us.

I *feel* he's still there, that he's much more than ashes in a pot – that he still has a presence and is as real as the tea and the toast. It's as though I expect him to break the silence at any moment with a sharp observation or two on the frailties of human nature or the lamentable state of the human condition. I sometimes say something out loud, as though to incite him to comment. Even when I think to myself, I'm fearful that my sentences may not be well formed or that I've chosen the wrong word. It's as though he's inside my mind ready to correct or admonish. And then I look up at the ceramic jar, almost expecting him to jump out in a puff of smoke like a genie from an Aladdin's lamp, take his place at the table, praise the quality of the brew and ask me to pass him another piece of toast.

What I just can't get over, and I think I never will, is how on earth Mr Potts could be flesh and blood one minute and a handful of ashes the next! How is it at all possible that a living, breathing, feeling, touching, thinking, talking, eating and drinking being can turn into mere dust and disappear into the air we breathe?! I've asked myself this question so many times that it's almost become an unrecognisable collection of words – just as a common enough word can sound nonsense if you repeat it over and over and over. But I think I can imagine what Mr Potts might say: 'But what *sort* of question is your question? It can't be a question of science, because you know how a tree can be cut down and turned to ash in a fire and become totally unrecognisable as a tree! It can be explained how one form of matter can be transformed into another. But would a scientific answer really *satisfy* you? If not, then maybe your question is not what it appears to be. Maybe you're not *asking* anything at all! But thanks anyway for *seeming* to ask.'

Yes, and once again he would leave me speechless. It would be as though he'd given me something wrapped up and told me not to unwrap it until I got home and until I felt in the right mood to do so, because I learned that I had to be in the right frame of mind to unwrap the cerebral presents Mr Potts gave me.

It's worthy of note, I think, that public opinion concerning Mr Potts underwent something of a short-term revision just after his demise – I will not say 'transformation', which is far too strong a word. I even overheard the phrase 'Poor Mr Potts' from the lips of his erstwhile critics. Gentler talk about him didn't last longer than the nine days customarily allotted to all who must shake off this mortal coil, except that Mr Potts was not simply a 'nine days' wonder' *after* his demise, but had been a wonder for a very long time in the eyes of cynical gossipers. The difference is that now the sting seemed to have been taken out, or at least diluted, amongst those who had viewed him as no more than an object of derision or as an eccentric best avoided if only because he had done his level best to avoid *them*! As a general observation, it's quite remarkable how even the most hated amongst humans while they live are yet capable of becoming almost respectable when they can no longer be regarded as any kind of threat. Another species of this remarkable transition is that people who were deprived of any praise or recognition when breathing suddenly become highly meritorious when deep in the cold ground or, like Mr Potts, when they are dust and floating through the air on which we all depend. Those whose talents were, rightly or wrongly, amply recognised while living are hoisted onto pedestals whose heights are envied by the gods, while those whose talents were either derided or ignored become worthy figures in the halls of fame. Such transformations are common enough amongst humans, but they are, I remember Mr Potts observing, very much frowned upon by the Elves, who believe that everyone must be truly judged and given just merit both in life and in death – human hypocrisy is one of those failings most detested by the Elves and by all those who believe in their existence and aspire to be more like them. In fact, I recall Mr Potts mentioning a conversation between two Elves, named Alpha and Beta, that he said he had overheard in one of his dreams and subsequently noted down, a snippet of which is quite apt here:

Alpha: The very best deserving are, while living,

Often shunned by the self-righteously unforgiving.

Beta:Yes, that pious crowd, I've heard it said,

Reserve their praises for the dead.

I might say that upon first hearing such expressions as 'Poor Mr Potts' I decided to wear ear plugs whenever I felt the need to leave the house. If only they had been kinder when he was amongst them he might have begun to believe more in them and less in the Elves – 'Better late than never' is a poor consolation, and none at all from the lips of hypocrites. I might also say that after nine days of wonder people began to look rather strangely at me and I sensed that they were giving me a wide berth (by which I mean, of course, that they were avoiding me and not that they were offering me a large bed or a small cabin to sleep in!) I also seemed to sense that they were talking behind my back, or whispering whenever they were obliged by necessity to come near me on narrow pavements. I even began to hear muffled chuckling. It was all very distasteful, but when I showed my distaste by frowning and keeping my distance, the whispering and the chuckling seemed to increase, as though I was unknowingly fanning the flames of an unwelcome fire. Perhaps they thought that any friend of Mr Potts, especially one who was living in his old house and refusing to renovate it, and one who was refusing to join with the local consensus in the former attitude towards Mr Potts, which, I felt, was beginning once again to rise like a hungry sea serpent from the depths of dark waters – well, in view of all this, perhaps they thought that I was thoroughly deserving of similar treatment. The upshot is that I keep very much to myself and have no expectation of meeting anyone in these parts, or any other parts, in whom I feel able to confide my deepest thoughts.

Well, that's how things are. I feel comfortable in Mr Potts's house, though there is something mightily strange and particular that I am determined to keep to myself.

Before I explain, let me say at once that I have decided to keep very much to myself, outside these pages, everything I know about Mr Potts. There's more than enough gossip about the poor fellow already, and I don't wish to fan the flames of derogatory gossip regarding his state of mind – his memory is very precious to me and I wish very much to keep it that way.

Anyway, what I'm especially concerned to keep to myself has to do with Elves. I have already recounted, if you remember, how, in my old house, I detected something odd in the spare room that caused me to speculate about the doings of Elves, especially after consulting with Mr Potts, who is, or rather *was*, something of an expert on the subject – worse luck for him, in the sense that it only added to the speculation surrounding his own sanity.

From the very first night I spent in my new home, I began to have the strangest of dreams – not nightmares, but dreams of a sort I'd never ever had before. In them, I could hear indistinct voices, as though speaking in a different language, but a language that was soft and mellow, and these voices seemed to me to express surprise and wonder, as though they belonged to people who were trying to understand a curiosity or some new thing. I say 'people', but their speech, though indistinct, didn't seem to match up in degree whatsoever with the different languages I'd been hearing all my life. So much for sound, for what I could hear. I could see also, and what I saw were slender, shadowy figures milling around in a woody place, shadows which had heads and arms and legs and wore clothes – but colours and detail I was unable to make out.

That's how it all started, and I've been having the same kind of dream several times a week. The rest of the time I sleep very soundly – my sleep is dreamless, something that I'd always wished for, because until now my sleep was troubled by nightmares of all descriptions, some remembered, some half remembered, and some, although forgotten on waking, left me disturbed, as though I hadn't slept at all but was forced to stare out the entire night in pitch blackness. Yes, the very best of my dreams left me mildly uneasy, and the worst, by far the majority, were deeply and lastingly disquieting. But now I have even begun to look forward to my dreams of shadowy figures talking about I know not what. Perhaps one day they'll begin to speak in a language I can understand – when they can trust me and know who and what I am. Until then, I wait in a 'penombra', a kind of half-light enjoyed by unconscionable thieves and modest heroes alike.

And, meanwhile, I can never forget Mr Potts.

I say I can never forget Mr Potts. The fact is, I can't *afford* to forget him. Allow me to explain.

For many, he was no more than an old duffer, a grumpy old eccentric with an infinite capacity for complaining. But just as love and grief are inevitable bedfellows in that you can't grieve for someone you've never loved, so too is just complaint inseparable from a deep sense of right and of justice. Mr Potts carried a torch without which the world of men would be a very much darker place. He carried a light which, like a baton, should be passed from stalwart hand to stalwart hand if all vestiges of hope are not to be entirely extinguished and, if the worlds of Elves and man are ever to lightly touch from time to time and from place to place. It's the kind of light that inspires those with courage despite the many tempests that batter their resolve and test their love of life and man. If it isn't going too far, I feel constrained to say that Mr Potts's life, or at least the portion of it I was lucky enough to be acquainted with, was a continuous cry in the wilderness. Unlike John the Baptist, Mr Potts's head was not violently removed from his body to appease the whim of a dancing girl, though I know of many who would not have lifted a finger to prevent Mr Potts's own decapitation, provided it didn't take place on a Sunday.

Anyway, that's why I can't afford to forget Mr Potts – he being a rare torch-bearer in a very dark place.

(By the way, when I say that Mr Potts was a torch-bearer, I don't of course mean that he was in the habit of holding aloft a fiery brand wherever he went, a practice which would have been dangerous to say the least and would have done very little to inspire the downhearted. What I mean is ... well, I think you must *know* what I mean. Also, to speak of a 'cry in the wilderness' does not mean that someone is shouting at the top of his voice in a very secluded place – what on earth would be the point of that, anyway? But again, surely no explanation is needed.)

Now another word about those delightful creatures, Elves. Suffice to say that some humans who feel that they and the world they inhabit are abandoned by their gods will look to the Elves for solace – and for some reassurance that what they imagine the Elves to be is not so far removed from what humans may in good time become.

Were I an Elf, what should I say about Mr Potts? Was he as crazy as many, if not most, said he was? Or was his own judgement that the rest of humanity is insane sufficient testament to his own sanity, albeit a sanity that was uncommonly uncomfortable? Was he like a teacher faced with an un-teachable class of pupils? Well then, no wonder that he sought solace under a warm blanket of eccentricity. Anyway, the very least we can say is that in a world in which a Judas would feel very much at home, he was not a Judas unto himself!

But, then, I am not an Elf – not quite or not yet, anyway. And if Elves are to be given the last word, this is something that can't be hurried. It must be remembered that my own commentary consists largely of impressions gleaned from my association with Mr Potts, and I must say that this association was not altogether pleasant. When you see in a glass darkly, what you see is always an impression half-formed and only half-enjoyed, as though you are glimpsing a parallel world in which you are not altogether welcome.

I await the judgement of Elves, but I am as confident as I can be that their assessment will be wise and fair.

With this, I say farewell to Mr Potts, with some regret that he did not people the world with little Potts-es. But, of course, there is no guarantee that his progeny would have followed his example, no guarantee at all – and, really, would we have wished upon them a similar fate?

Every evening, when the sun goes down and the birds in the nearby trees have gone to rest, I sit and wait in shadow-filled places, perhaps as Mr Potts himself did, wrapped all about only in the music of trees – sitting and waiting, waiting and sitting. Waiting. The question 'Waiting for *what*? is one that can be asked in as many ways as it can be meant – which, as Mr Potts would insist, is another way of saying that it is not at all an ordinary question, and one that tells us more about the questioner than anything else. But that's Mr Potts! I am myself in no way competent to comment further.

Chapter Eighteen

MARTIANS ... AND CYNICS

I've said that Mr Potts is dead. Being dead is, in the natural course of things, no achievement. But living in the full knowledge of the very worst one's fellow human beings are capable of, and being extraordinarily sensitive to begin with, is quite another matter, I would say.

Well, in view of Mr Potts's very extraordinary, I might even say extra-terrestrial sensitivities, I really did begin to wonder whether he was actually a Martian who had unaccountably found himself stranded on planet Earth and unable to return. All he could have done is observe his surroundings and all those humans around him, watch and learn, and wait for a rescue that would never come. Poor fellow! – if I can use this expression for a Martian.

In making his observations and in basing his judgements upon them, he might of course have got things wrong, or out of perspective, so to speak. Even so, he would never have been too far from the mark and he should be given the highest praise for attempting to hit the bullseye even if he never quite managed it. After all, who on earth can be trusted to give a full and true account of the human condition and all its possible ramifications? No human I can think of, for even the very best of humans are flawed and far too close to events to see the wood for the trees. And it really would take the very best of them to be moved sufficiently to take on the task. There again, even if Martians exist, who's to say that they could be entrusted with the task or that their observations would be more accurate or their judgements more reasoned and reasonable?

If I myself were a Martian ... well I should in all likelihood be quite lost for words. If I wrote things down about human beings, the words I write on one page might be complementary and gracious, but on the next they might be most reproving and dismissive. The whole idea of being a Martian and commenting upon the beings who inhabit planet Earth is quite a puzzle, and really very little can be done with it. But the point is that I did foolishly entertain the idea that Mr Potts was secretly in communication with some higher, extra-terrestrial authority.

On the other hand, I might just as well argue that Mr Potts was simply too eccentric and too passionate to be anything other than *human*! For who could possibly be in a position to hold humans so thoroughly to account for their misdeeds if not one of their very own? Isn't it necessary to be human to understand humans? If so, there is some glimmer of hope that humans may one day be saved by one or more of their own kind.

All this is, of course, quite beyond my own mind skills to understand properly or to work out, and it's at times like this when I miss Mr Potts most, because he would be sure to say something profound and vastly illuminating even if I failed, as usual, to understand it.

I must confess, I find myself at a total loss to sum things up adequately. But I think I can say something about *cynicism*. I've sometimes heard it said that Mr Potts was no more than a 'cynical old recluse', and those who say this sort of thing are even trying to be kind, stopping short of saying something they consider even far less complimentary. They believe, as almost everyone does, that cynicism is something necessarily lamentable, and, for once, they have language and word-sense on their side. But a cynic is a species of critic, and he may be a critic with very important things to say, and a cynical remark may galvanise others to action much more effectively than clichés of praise.

Perhaps we should take a longer, harder look at this thing called 'cynicism', for if someone has heard and read about the very worst that humans do to one another, and even *seen* what they do, cynicism may well be a natural result – I mean, cynicism may well be the product of bleeding heart destitute of all hope that humans will ever stop doing the worst things that they do. If this is true, then the seat of cynicism must be a love profound and inexhaustible and a belief in the unimpeachable sanctity of human life, for such a love and such a belief can never acquiesce in man's inhumanity to man.

I don't know, of course, but this brief and inadequate account of cynicism might seem to follow from a remark once made by Mr Potts in an address he made to an imaginary gathering of the Senate of ancient Rome. Wrapped in a more than generous bath towel, he declared, his right arm pointing accusingly to his audience:

'Scorn not the cynic, for from heaven he comes and to heaven he will return!'

Perhaps he would forgive me for not now knowing whether I should write 'heaven' with a small letter or a capital, but, anyway, these were his words as far as I remember them – and I think I remember them very well, because I shall never forget that huge, stripy bath-towel which seemed at the time to give his words additional weight, so that the bath-towel and the words are, as it were, inextricably linked, the one an indelible *aide memoir* to the other, so to speak.

Now if Mr Potts was indeed such a cynic in his attitude towards grave human injustice and cruelty, it might explain why the Elves, although they sadly missed him, never once shed a tear over his demise – or so I have quite recently learned and can well believe. It's as though, coming from heaven and then returning to it, he simply went home to stay! Is heaven a place, then? Why, no! Maybe it's more akin to an idea, and those who partake in it while they live can only make it stronger and more indestructible by returning to it when their time on this planet is up. But I'm not so sure about the word 'returning'. No, I should like to think that my friend Mr

Potts has been 're-absorbed' into an idea and that the idea is much the better for that. *What* idea, exactly? Well, I'm not at all sure that it's possible to be *exact* about such things, but I would say that it's the idea of a profound and, maybe for many people, inexplicable kind of love – a love of humans *despite* the worst they do to one another. Do I make myself obscure? I sincerely hope so, for there is nothing more obscure than discussions concerning human nature, human behaviour and the whys and the wherefores of the human condition. Now Mr Potts had little sympathy with obscurity, as I hope I have made clear – yet this is one kind of obscurity I really believe he might excuse.

(As a final note touching the importance of the correct use of language, Mr Potts would no doubt reproach me for my saying that something might be 'more indestructible'. I can hear him whispering in my ear that a thing is either indestructible or it is not, that the concept of indestructibility cannot admit of degrees. What's more, when I say I think of him as being 're-absorbed', he would be quick to remind me about the tricks and illusions involved in the pictures evoked by the use and abuse of figurative language. Well, alright. I'm happy to leave the last word to him.)

Well, almost the last word. It has occurred to me that my remarks about Mr Potts might be unread, or read but unconsidered, or considered but quickly forgotten, so that all my efforts to preserve his memory have been a waste of time. And then, I recall his words, 'All time is a waste of time, but the trick is how to waste it most usefully,' a sentiment that leaves me with the limping hope that I have at least wasted time usefully, though I struggle, once again, to understand what he could possibly have meant.

But, you see, he has the last word after all.

Perhaps I may be permitted my own very last word. Those who have said that Mr Potts never really 'lived' (note the inverted commas) are in the relevant sense quite right. In a world that suffers from the cheap cult of mere celebrity and its soul-mate elevated mediocrity, Mr Potts failed miserably and consistently. But he merits the title Noble Failure. If he failed in all things which most people covet and define as 'success', he did so with a nobility that is very rare indeed, a nobility which permits him free access to a heaven he could not discover amongst his fellows. For it is far better to be a noble failure than an undeserved success.

* * * * *

ND - #0318 - 270225 - C0 - 234/156/11 - PB - 9781780916347 - Gloss Lamination